W9-BRE-750

"Good Night, Mitch. Sweet Dreams."

Tori stood on tiptoe and kissed his cheek.

The sweetest dream was in his arms, but he wouldn't make a move now. If she wanted to be friendly, he could do that. At least tonight. "Night, Tori."

Again, neither of them moved away. Tori grabbed his neck and brought his lips to hers.

As far as kisses went, this one had little to do with simple friendship. Simple need, yes. It was hot. It was deep. It was killing Mitch not to take it further.

Tori pushed away first and Mitch held up his palms. "That was not my fault."

She slid both hands through her hair. "I know. It was mine. It won't happen again."

Mitch headed for the door, but before he walked out, he turned to her and said, "You just keep telling yourself that, Tori. Maybe then you'll start to believe it."

Dear Reader,

Welcome to another fabulous month at Silhouette Desire, where we offer you the best in passionate, powerful and provocative love stories. You'll want to delve right in to our latest DYNASTIES: THE DANFORTHS title with Anne Marie Winston's highly dramatic *The Enemy's Daughter*—you'll never guess who the latest Danforth bachelor has gotten involved with! And the steam continues to rise when Annette Broadrick returns to the Desire line with a brand-new series, THE CRENSHAWS OF TEXAS. These four handsome brothers will leave you breathless, right from the first title, *Branded.*

Read a Silhouette Desire novel from *his* point of view in our new promotion MANTALK. Eileen Wilks continues this series with her highly innovative and intensely emotional story *Meeting at Midnight.* Kristi Gold continues her series THE ROYAL WAGER with another confirmed bachelor about to meet his match in *Unmasking the Maverick Prince.* How comfortable can *A Bed of Sand* be? Well, honey, if you're lying on it with the hero of Laura Wright's latest novel…who cares! And the always enjoyable Roxanne St. Claire, whom *Publishers Weekly* calls "an author who's on the fast track to making her name a household one," is scorching up the pages with *The Fire Still Burns.*

Happy reading,

Melissa Jeglinski

Melissa Jeglinski
Senior Editor, Silhouette Desire

Please address questions and book requests to:
Silhouette Reader Service
U.S.: 3010 Walden Ave., P.O. Box 1325, Buffalo, NY 14269
Canadian: P.O. Box 609, Fort Erie, Ont. L2A 5X3

UNMASKING THE MAVERICK PRINCE

KRISTI GOLD

Silhouette®
Desire
Published by Silhouette Books
America's Publisher of Contemporary Romance

If you purchased this book without a cover you should be aware that this book is stolen property. It was reported as "unsold and destroyed" to the publisher, and neither the author nor the publisher has received any payment for this "stripped book."

SILHOUETTE BOOKS

ISBN 0-373-76606-8

UNMASKING THE MAVERICK PRINCE

Copyright © 2004 by Kristi Goldberg

All rights reserved. Except for use in any review, the reproduction or utilization of this work in whole or in part in any form by any electronic, mechanical or other means, now known or hereafter invented, including xerography, photocopying and recording, or in any information storage or retrieval system, is forbidden without the written permission of the editorial office, Silhouette Books, 233 Broadway, New York, NY 10279 U.S.A.

All characters in this book have no existence outside the imagination of the author and have no relation whatsoever to anyone bearing the same name or names. They are not even distantly inspired by any individual known or unknown to the author, and all incidents are pure invention.

This edition published by arrangement with Harlequin Books S.A.

® and TM are trademarks of Harlequin Books S.A., used under license. Trademarks indicated with ® are registered in the United States Patent and Trademark Office, the Canadian Trade Marks Office and in other countries.

Visit Silhouette Books at www.eHarlequin.com

Printed in U.S.A.

Books by Kristi Gold

Silhouette Desire

Cowboy for Keeps #1308
Doctor for Keeps #1320
His Sheltering Arms #1350
Her Ardent Sheikh #1358
Dr. Dangerous #1415
Dr. Desirable #1421
Dr. Destiny #1427
His E-Mail Order Wife #1454
The Sheikh's Bidding #1485
Renegade Millionaire #1497
Marooned with a Millionaire #1517
Expecting the Sheikh's Baby #1531
Fit for a Sheikh #1576
Challenged by the Sheikh #1586
†*Persuading the Playboy King* #1600
†*Unmasking the Maverick Prince* #1606

*Marrying an M.D.
†The Royal Wager

KRISTI GOLD

has always believed that love has remarkable healing powers and feels very fortunate to be able to weave stories of romance and commitment. As a bestselling author and a Romance Writers of America RITA® Award finalist, she's learned that although accolades are wonderful, the most cherished rewards come from personal stories shared by readers.

You can reach Kristi at KGOLDAUTHOR@aol.com, through her Web site at kristigold.com or by snail mail at P.O. Box 9070, Waco, Texas 76714. (Please include an SASE for a response.)

To the Ditzy Chix, the greatest group of authors on earth,
for their wonderful camaraderie. And to the Chix-a-Dees,
a fantastic group of romance readers whose commitment
to the genre never ceases to amaze me.
Thanks to you all for your continued support.

Prologue

Tomorrow morning, Mitchell Edward Warner III planned to get the hell out of Harvard and return to the Oklahoma cattle ranch where he'd spent every summer since his birth. The place where he'd been taught to ride a horse and rope a steer without breaking too many bones. Where at fifteen, he'd fumbled his way through sex with a country girl down by the creek, high on adrenaline and teenage lust, as well as the prospect of getting caught. By the summer of his eighteenth year, he'd gotten pretty damn good at all three.

But he'd never been any good at being what his father wanted him to be—the heir apparent of a dynasty spanning four generations of high-powered politicians. He'd made the decision to shun his legacy, first by rejecting the preferred Texas alma mater in favor of an Ivy League school, and then going further against tradition by choosing business over law. He refused to enter the world of partisan politics and social-climbing suck-ups where both his father and betrayal reigned supreme.

The hoots and hollers filtering in from outside made Mitch long for a freedom that still wasn't quite within his reach. Instead, he was hidden away with two friends, Marc DeLoria and Dharr Halim, in their shared apartment. An unlikely trio to most observers, but they had one very important thing in common—unwelcome attention from the press because of family ties. Tonight was no different from the rest. Sons of kings and senators had a hard time remaining invisible.

While the post-graduation party raged outside, Mitch claimed his favorite spot on the floor with his back to the wall, appropriate since at times he felt that way in a very real sense. He tossed aside the ranching magazine he'd pretended to be reading and picked up the champagne bottle to refill his glass, wishing it were a beer. "We've already toasted our success. Now I suggest we toast a long bachelorhood." He topped off Dharr's and Marc's drinks, replaced the bottle in the bucket and then held up his glass.

Dharr raised his flute. "I would most definitely toast to that."

Marc hesitated, champagne in hand, and after a few moments said, "I prefer to propose a wager."

Dharr and Mitch glanced at each other before turning their attention back to Marc. "What kind of wager, DeLoria?" Mitch asked.

"Well, since we've all agreed that we're not ready for marriage in the immediate future, if ever, I suggest we hold ourselves to those terms by wagering we'll all be unmarried on our tenth reunion."

"And if we are not?" Dharr asked.

"We'll be forced to give away our most prized possession."

Oh, hell. Mitch could only think of one thing, something he valued more than any material object he had ever owned, and he'd owned plenty. "Give away my gelding? That would be tough."

Dharr looked even less enthusiastic when he glanced at the

painting hanging above Mitch's head. "I suppose that would be my Modigliani, and I must admit that giving away the nude would cause me great suffering."

"That's the point, gentlemen," Marc said. "The wager would mean nothing if the possessions were meaningless."

Mitch found it kind of strange that Marc hadn't mentioned anything he would be willing to give away. "Okay, DeLoria. What's it going to be for you?"

"The Corvette."

Damn, that vehicle was legendary, and Mitch had a hard time believing Marc would actually part with it. "You'd give up the love mobile?"

"Of course not. I won't lose."

"Nor will I," Dharr said. "Ten years will be adequate before I am forced to adhere to an arranged marriage in order to produce an heir."

"No problem for me," Mitch said, and it wasn't. "I'm going to avoid marriage at all costs."

Again Dharr held up his glass. "Then we are all agreed?"

Mitch touched his flute to Dharr's. "Agreed."

Marc did the same. "Let the wager begin."

Mitch smiled, the first sincere one in days. Team players to the end.

Without a doubt, Mitch would beat them all. Marc was too damn fond of women not to get caught in someone's trap. Dharr would probably buckle under his father's pressure and marry the woman chosen for him. Which left Mitch to do what he did best—stand on his own.

He figured the press would eventually get tired of stalking him if he didn't give them anything to talk about. He would blend into the real world in a single-stoplight town where people didn't look at him like he were some kind of a god. He'd get rid of every suit he'd ever owned, spend his days in jeans and chaps and his nights in the local bar, with women who didn't expect anything but a few turns on the dance floor and an occasional good time after closing.

And if he was lucky, he'd finally be left alone to live his life as he pleased, however he pleased, and finally walk into a place without being noticed.

One

Nine years later.

When he strode through the doors with all the self-assurance of a living legend, Victoria Barnett almost dropped her plastic cup of cheap chardonnay into her lap.

The pair of Wranglers washed out in places too difficult to ignore, the denim shirt pushed up at the sleeves revealing tanned forearms covered by a veneer of dark hair and the black Resistol tipped low on his brow gave the appearance that he was any hard-working, testosterone-laden cowboy searching for a way to spend a Friday night—probably between the sheets.

But he wasn't just any cowboy. He was Quail Run's favored son, the next best thing to American royalty, and Tori's possible ticket to a pay raise and promotion.

The journalist in her reacted with excitement at the prospect of obtaining the story of the decade. The woman in her reacted with heat to his diamond-blue eyes assessing the crowd with guarded interest as he worked his way to the jam-packed bar.

A few men acknowledged his presence with a casual, "Hey, Mitch," as if his appearance in this dusty down-home dive was a common occurrence. More than a few women eyed him as if he were the answer to their wildest dreams.

Tori couldn't imagine why a man of his caliber would frequent a place like Sadler's Bar and Grill, or choose to reside in this unforgiving southern Oklahoma town. Had it not been for her best friend's upcoming wedding, Tori would never have returned to Quail Run, where she'd grown up in hand-me-downs and a hard-luck shack. Poor little Tori, whose mama hadn't bothered to marry her dad—not that he'd bothered to ask.

But for the first time in two days, she was glad she had come back. And if luck prevailed, Mitch Warner would give her exactly what she needed.

"You really should give it a whirl, Tori."

Tori turned to her right and gave her attention to Stella Moore, the reason for her presence in the local bar—a final girlfriend get-together before Stella married Bobby Lehman tomorrow night. "Give what a whirl?"

Stella nodded toward the small stage at the front of the dance floor where some bearded, beer-bellied deejay wearing a T-shirt that read Bite Me was setting up for karaoke. "You should sing. You know you want to."

"Just do it, Tori," Janie Young said with an added nudge in Tori's left side. "Plainie Janie" as she'd been known in school. But with her waist-length blond hair, perfectly made-up green eyes and lithe five-foot, eleven-inch frame, Tori concluded that Janie couldn't lay claim to being plain now. On the contrary, her chosen career involved gracing the runways from New York to Paris as a renowned model known simply as Jada.

"One of you can sing," Tori said. "I'd rather sit here and finish my wine." Even if it was really bad wine.

"Come on, Tori," Stella cajoled. "You had the best voice in the high school choir. Show it off."

A hot blush crawled up Tori's throat and settled on her cheeks. "That's not saying all that much, considering there were only ten of us in the choir."

Janie frowned. "Don't put yourself down. You know you're talented. Besides, it'll be good practice before you sing at the wedding tomorrow night."

Tori grabbed a lock of hair and twirled it round and round her finger, a nervous habit she'd begun at the age of three, when she'd finally acquired some hair, according to her mom. Back when her mom still remembered all the little milestones in her daughter's life, before she'd forgotten her only child's name. Back when her mom was still around.

Pushing away the sadness, Tori said, "It's been a long time since I've sung in public." A long time since she'd had anything to sing about.

Brianne McIntyre returned to the table from the restroom, her red curls bouncing in time with her exuberant stride, completing the "Fearsome Foursome," as they'd labeled themselves during their youth. Another of the prodigal daughters who rarely returned home, Brianne resided in Houston where she was currently attending her third college and studying nursing, still undecided on what she wanted to be when she grew up.

Something sinister was stirring, Tori decided, when her friends displayed some fairly devious smiles. "What are you three up to now?"

Stella rested a hand on her belly, slightly swollen from the pregnancy that had been the reason for the hurry-up wedding. "Nothing at all, Tori. We're just here to have some fun."

Stella's assertions did nothing to silence the suspicion running at full steam in Tori's head.

Janie leaned forward and grinned. "Don't look now, girls, but Mitch Warner's sitting at a table on the other side of the dance floor."

Tori didn't dare look again. Not unless she wanted to be totally obvious in her admiration. "I know. I saw him come in."

Janie, however, opted to be obvious and fairly drooled after turning back to the group. "Oh my gosh, what I wouldn't do to that man if I had the chance. He's hotter than an Oklahoma sidewalk in August."

So was Tori, thanks to Mitch Warner, even it was October, not August, and forty degrees outside. "He's okay."

"Okay?" Stella's hazel eyes went almost as wide as the round table where they were seated. "He's drop-dead gorgeous. And last week, Bobby told me he and Mary Alice Marshall finally broke up. She's going to marry Brady the banker."

Brianne wrinkled her freckled nose. "I still can't believe he was dating her. Everyone knows she's slept with every cowboy under thirty in this town."

All three of them, Tori thought wryly.

Stella shook her head, sending her dark curls into a dance as she sent Brianne a warning look that wasn't lost on Tori. "No one knows that for sure, Brianne. People here are too judgmental for their own good."

Tori considered that to be a colossal understatement. The town's residents had said the same thing about her own mother many times, which was probably the reason for Stella's scolding. Or maybe Stella's unplanned pregnancy had sent the rumor mill back into full swing.

"The way I understand it, she and Mitch did the deed the first time one summer over fifteen years ago," Janie said in a conspiratorial whisper. "They've been on and off, literally, since he came back here to live."

Tori had heard about Mitch's and Mary Alice's extracurricular activities when she'd still been living in Quail Run, but she'd been too young to care. Five years her senior, Mitch Warner had been the elusive, enigmatic rich boy who'd only come to town during the summer. And she'd only caught a glimpse of him a time or two when she'd been riding her bike and seen the limousine drive past on the way to his maternal grandfather's ranch. During those times, she'd found the car much more fascinating than him.

Besides, boys like Mitch Warner hadn't been interested in Tori

Barnett, who'd lived on the wrong side of the social dividing line. Even though she could have spent her days ostracized from the mainstream and hanging her head in shame, she hadn't. Instead, she'd graduated valedictorian, worked her way through college and now struggled to establish herself at the Dallas women's magazine, where she currently served as a staff reporter.

An interview with a revered United States senator's reclusive son could propel her career to unknown heights, and provide much-needed money. She might even be able to pay off the bills she'd incurred when her mother had been in the hospital. If Mitch Warner cooperated.

"Yoo-hoo, are you in there, Victoria?"

Tori snapped to and stared blankly at Janie. "I was just thinking."

Brianne presented a wily grin. "About Mitch Warner?"

As a matter of fact. Tori finger-combed her bangs, surprised they weren't cemented to her forehead because of the perspiration gathering there. "Just thinking about work."

Stella blew a raspberry between her full lips. "Stop thinking about work, and try to enjoy yourself. I am, even if I can't have anything fun to drink."

Reminded of her own drink, Tori took a quick swallow of the less-than-palatable wine. "Okay, I promise I'll have some fun. But I'm not going to sing."

"Our first singer tonight is Tori Barnett, one of Quail Run's own, so let's give her a big Sadler welcome back!"

Tori sent her friends a bitter look and didn't bother to budge, even when the deejay called her name again.

"Get up there, Victoria May," Janie insisted, followed by several patrons chanting, "To-ri! To-ri!"

Making a total fool of herself in front of her friends was the very last thing Tori wanted at the moment. And more important, making a fool of herself in front of Mitch Warner wouldn't help her cause. But she hadn't forgotten how to sing, so she might as well meet the challenge head-on.

After all, what was the worst thing that could happen?

Tori confronted the worst thing when she stepped up on the stage, took her place behind the microphone and realized her brain had gone back to the table.

She knew the Patsy Cline song by heart, but this would be a nightmare, not a sweet dream, if she couldn't choke out the words now lodged in her throat, because Mitch Warner—kicked back in the chair, a beer wrapped in his large hands and the full extent of his blue, blue eyes and jet-black hair revealed because he'd removed his hat—had chosen that very moment to smile at her.

Tori felt naked under his perusal, totally exposed and definitely warm. As the song's intro began a second time, she had only one thought. If she couldn't sing in front of him, she'd never have the nerve to ask him for an interview.

That alone drove her to close her eyes and open her mouth to perform in public for the first time in years. She might have momentarily forgotten the lyrics, but she would never forget that Harvard cowboy's perfect smile.

Mitch Warner had never seen an angel dressed in black leather.

That's exactly how she sounded, this woman named Tori—like an angel. But she looked like a passport to sin. It wasn't her voice that made him imagine her beneath him, naked, her long legs wrapped around his waist, her silky brown hair brushing over his chest as they took a slow trip to heaven. And he'd probably go straight to hell in a handbasket if he decided to act on that fantasy. But as his gaze tracked the snug leather pants that showcased her curves and her breasts that rose beneath the form-fitting red turtleneck sweater with each breath she took, Mitch engaged in a battle below his belt buckle that he wasn't sure he could win.

When he'd entered the bar, he'd planned to stay only long enough to meet his foreman and rescue him from an all-day drinking binge in honor of the end of his bachelorhood. He didn't care for crowds or socializing except when necessary. Trust wasn't something that came easily for him. He never knew when some member of the press might be lurking in the shadows, waiting to catch him doing something that might be deemed newsworthy. For that reason, he was reluctant to talk to strangers.

But tonight…. Well, tonight he might make an exception with this stranger named Tori. Bobby could find another ride home since Mitch planned to meet the woman responsible for his current predicament. Whatever happened after that was anyone's guess.

He gave his full attention to Tori, who was now singing the final chorus. It was all Mitch could do to keep his boots firmly planted on the floor when she smiled, tossed a long lock of hair over her shoulder and then left the stage. He hadn't done this in a long time, but he remembered enough to know that appearing too eager would most likely turn her off.

He waited for two more singers to finish—if you could call drunken geezers, who couldn't carry a tune in a front-end loader, singers. A slow ballad now played on the jukebox, providing the opportunity to have Tori polish his belt buckle. Damn, he didn't need to think about that. Otherwise he'd have to remain seated indefinitely.

After finishing the last of his beer, Mitch replaced his hat, stood and worked his way across the dance floor crowded with mostly married couples, since the town still held true to a strict moral code. And those who ignored the code maintained rooms by the hour at the Quail Run Court.

He arrived at the table to find his foreman's fiancée, Stella, sitting with two other pretty ladies whom Mitch didn't know, nor did he want to know them. His interest was tuned solely into the singing angel who kept her gaze centered on the empty plastic cup clutched in her hand.

"Hey, Mitch," Stella said. "I thought you might be with Bobby out at the Greers' ranch, drinking yourself into a stupor."

"No time for that." Mitch kept his eyes trained on Tori who had yet to look at him. "We're getting ready to move the cattle into the south pasture before the first real norther hits."

The redhead bent her elbows and braced her jaw on her palms. "Isn't it kind of early for that, since it's only October?"

"Nope," Mitch said, and left it at that. He didn't have the desire to explain the workings of a cattle ranch or the weather to this particular woman. He only had the desire to get this brown-haired angel into his arms to see if her body felt as good as it looked. "Care to dance, Tori?"

Her gaze zipped to his and she looked as if he'd asked her to strip naked. "Are you talking to me?"

"Unless there's someone else named Tori at the table."

She stared at the hand he offered like he'd grown claws. "It's been a long time since I've danced."

"It's been a long time since you've sung, too," Stella said. "I doubt you've forgotten that, either. And even if you have, I'm sure Mitch would be glad to show you how, wouldn't you Mitch?"

"I can do that." He'd be glad to show her a lot of moves, none that he'd dare undertake in public. First things first. Right now, he had to get her away from the table and onto the dance floor.

She finally stood, but didn't take his hand. She did follow him to the middle of the floor, where Mitch faced her and took her palm to rest in his palm and then circled his other arm around her shoulders. She linked two fingers of her free hand on to his belt loop, like she was afraid to really touch him. Hopefully she would relax after a while, once she realized Mitch was only interested in dancing. For now.

Despite the fact they weren't that close, Mitch might as well have been covered from head to toe by a goose down blanket, not denim, considering he was quickly warming up. She could dance better than most and he imagined her skills were far-reaching. But that was all he could do—imagine—since she continued to maintain a safe distance.

She also refused to look at him until he said, "I'm Mitch."

"I know who you are."

Damn. He'd hoped she didn't know, but he shouldn't be all that surprised. His notoriety had followed him to Oklahoma, even if the media attention had waned over the past few years. But that was subject to change at any given moment, especially if the rumors about his father's retirement were true. Then it would start all over again, the speculation about whether Mitch would step in and take up the political reins. That would be a hot day in Antarctica. The only reins Mitch cared about were attached to a horse's bridle.

He decided to focus on something more pleasant, namely the woman with the big brown eyes who was sort of in his arms. He figured if he drew her into a conversation then maybe he could work his way in to drawing her closer. "How long have you lived in Quail Run?"

"I don't live here."

That disappointed the hell out of Mitch. "But the karaoke guy said—"

"I'm one of Quail Run's own, I know." And she didn't sound too pleased by that fact. "I grew up here, but I've been gone for almost ten years. I moved to Norman to go to college after I graduated from high school."

About the same time Mitch had come back from Harvard. "So what brings you to town?"

She lowered her eyes again. "Stella's wedding. I'm her maid of honor."

At least they had something in common. "Oh, yeah? I'm Bobby's man of honor."

The comment earned him her full attention and the full effect of a smile that threatened to knock the sawdust floor from beneath his boots. "Not the best man?" she asked.

"Not in Stella's opinion."

Her smile disappeared. "You and Stella dated?"

"Hell, no!" He hadn't meant to say that with such force, but that's all he needed, a rumor he'd bedded his friend's fiancée. That would be enough to send the rag reporters running back to Quail Run. "Stella's only a friend. She wanted Bobby to ask her brother to stand up for him. He picked me instead."

"I can't really blame Bobby. If I had to choose between

you and Clint Moore, I'd have to say you would be my choice."

"You have something against Clint?"

She frowned. "I have something against guys who can't control their hands in movie theaters."

Mitch wondered if that rule applied to guys on dance floors. At least he'd been forewarned. "So you dated Clint Moore?"

"I dodged Clint Moore. I'm basing my opinion on hearsay, and that's probably not fair at all. I'm sure Clint's really a nice guy beneath that playboy exterior."

"Are you dating anyone now?" *Good, Mitch. Nothing like being subtle.*

She shrugged. "I don't have time to date."

That pleased Mitch. Nothing stood in his way of seeing her again, at least while she was still in town, if she was willing. "What takes up your time?"

"Mainly work."

"What do you do for a living? Sing?"

"No."

"Then what?"

She looked away and sighed. "I really don't want to talk about my work right now. I'm trying to forget about it. Besides, I'd only bore you."

He doubted anything involving her mouth would bore him. "What do you want to talk about?"

She gave him another energetic smile, which also gave Mitch a rush that went straight to his head. "Tell me about you," she said.

Mitch wasn't sure he wanted to go there. "What about me?"

"I want to know what it's like to live on a working ranch."

At least she hadn't asked what it was like to be a revered politician's son. Mitch would have two words to describe that—pure hell.

They talked for only a minute until the karaoke resumed with a few more wannabes trying their hand at singing in voices that could rouse dead driftwood. Frustrated, Mitch showed

Tori to a table in the corner near the dance floor and away from the crowd to continue the conversation.

The noise in the bar seemed to fade away as they turned the discussion to their favorite pastimes. He learned that Tori loved riding horses, and he told her about his prize gelding, Ray. She asked about his grandfather but never asked about his father, and he appreciated that more than she knew. He liked the way her laughter sounded when he told a joke, liked the way she twisted a strand of her hair when she described her disdain for Dallas traffic and big-city hassles. And it suddenly struck him that he'd told her more about himself in an hour than he'd told anyone in a lifetime. At least those aspects of his life he was willing to reveal.

After a while, Mitch moved to the seat next to her to hear her better, or so he'd told her, when in fact, the bar had quieted down after the karaoke had ended. In reality, he wanted to be close to her. He wasn't having a damn bit of trouble hearing her, but he was having one helluva time not touching her.

When a slow-dance tune filtered through the overhead speakers from the jukebox, Tori sighed and sent him another smile. "Gosh, I love this song."

He loved the way her dark eyes sparkled with pleasure. He imagined they would probably do the same when it came to a different kind of pleasure. And man, he'd like to find out. "Do you want to dance again?"

"Sure."

This time, Tori didn't hesitate coming to her feet or taking his hand to pull him up—not that he was resisting.

Mitch normally preferred something a little livelier than a love song, but he didn't mind at all when Tori didn't bother with his belt loop and instead, brought her arm around his back and laid her head against his chest.

He doubted she was much more than five foot five, and since he was six foot three, her head fit perfectly beneath his chin. Her hair smelled like flowers despite the fact the bar was hazy with smoke. Her body pressed against his brought back the desire in a rush of heat.

He slid his hand down her back to the dip of her spine but didn't dare go any farther, considering her comment about guys with roving hands. He didn't want to be put in the same class with Clint Moore. Besides, he wasn't a teenager anymore, and he didn't have to resort to blatant seduction to gain a woman's attention. He'd learned a long time ago not only how to satisfy a woman, but also how to read the signs. So far, Tori's body language told him she was comfortable only with dancing.

But that only lasted for the next two songs. By the third ballad, the first of a series of tunes involving torrid affairs in tangled sheets, things started to heat up between them. Mitch felt it in the way Tori's body dissolved into his, knew it when he moved his hand to her hip and she didn't protest.

They soon abandoned traditional country-dance form and wrapped their arms completely around each other. Their bodies touched in all the right places—her full breasts to his chest, thighs to thighs, pelvis to pelvis. Their hands roved over each other's backs where dampness had formed from the heat of the bar, the heat of their close proximity, the heat of the fire building between them.

Mitch let her go long enough to shed his denim shirt and hat, leaving him wearing only a plain white tee. Tori followed suit, removing the black leather jacket to reveal the sleeveless red sweater that formed to her breasts perfectly.

They left what clothes they could discard in public piled on the table, while Mitch imagined removing the rest of their clothes and taking her to his bed, beneath the patchwork quilt where he could end this torture. Where he could touch her with his hands, taste her with his mouth, satisfy the unbearable pressure building in his groin. But he had no right to ask that of her, even if he wanted her so badly he could carry her out of here at the first sign that she wanted it, too.

They came back together, moved together but remained mostly in one spot, in the corner away from the rest of the dancers, only occasionally drifting into another couple's path, disregarding the muttered cautions and the occasional near-collision.

Mitch buried his face in her neck, tested the shell of her ear with the tip of his tongue. She responded with a soft, pleasurable sound that drove Mitch wild. He nudged her bottom toward him with his palms, until not an inch separated their lower bodies and only one thing could bring them closer. If Tori, with the sweet sexy smile, the voice like an angel and the body that could turn Mitch into a devil, hadn't known how this unconventional foreplay was affecting Mitch down south, she did now. No way could she ignore his aroused state. No way could he ignore it, either, though he realized it was best if he tried.

God, he wanted to kiss her, but he wasn't sure whether to take the chance. If he made the move too soon, she might hightail it out of there, and he couldn't stand it if she did. First of all, he'd lose his dignity, considering he was hard as a horseshoe and was relying on Tori to hide that fact. Secondly, he didn't want this time to end without eventually knowing how her sexy mouth would feel against his, engaged in something besides small talk, even if that's all he would know tonight.

Maybe someone would play a fast song, something to help him regain control of his libido. He was surprised someone hadn't, but when he glanced at the jukebox and found Stella and her friends feeding in quarters and giving him a thumbs-up, he realized they'd been the reason behind the barrage of sex songs.

Then Tori tilted her face up, her warm lips settling against his neck, and Mitch gave up the fight. He danced her toward the dark, recessed area near the far end of the room, lit only by a flickering beer sign and far away from what was left of the late-night crowd.

Once they stepped off the floor, he guided her to the corner and backed her up against the wall. He braced one hand over her head and the other on her waist, angling his lower body away from her, at least for the time being. Her eyes, dark as a desert at midnight, looked hazy as he brushed a kiss over her forehead.

"Mitch, this is crazy," she said in a breathless whisper.

He trailed kisses along her jaw. "I know. Real crazy."

She turned her head slightly, giving him access to her neck. "We probably shouldn't do this."

He pressed fully against her once more, letting her know his body didn't agree. "Yeah. We probably shouldn't."

"Mitch," she murmured when he worked his mouth up her throat.

He lifted his head and palmed her face with one hand, running his thumb along her soft lower lip. "Yeah?"

She closed her eyes. "It's hot in here."

It was now or never. He chose now. "Do you want to go someplace else?"

"I want you to kiss me."

She didn't have to tell him twice. He lowered his lips to hers, only a breath away from finally having what he wanted from her now—what he'd wanted all damn night since the moment he'd laid eyes on her—until, "Get the hell away from my woman!" drew him away from her to look around the corner.

Bobby Lehman stood by the table where Stella was seated, his fists raised and aimed at the hulking deejay named Carl, a man who was twice the ranch foreman's size with a temper second only to a raging bull defending his herd.

Mitch could stay here and do what he wanted to do—kiss Tori senseless.

Or he could rescue the groom from getting a beating the night before his wedding.

Damn Bobby Lehman for ruining his night.

Two

Twenty minutes later, Tori found herself crammed into the front seat of Mitch's fifteen-year-old faded black truck. She was closest to the passenger door while Bobby Lehman, the big burr in her butt, occupied the place where Tori preferred to be—next to Mitch. But when Bobby had threatened to throw himself out of the truck after they'd pulled away from the bar, Tori had agreed to switch places and block the exit, saving Bobby from the clutches of concrete even if he had insisted, loudly, that he had to go after Stella. However, at the moment, Tori would gladly open the door and shove him out, doing them all a favor.

She'd never really understood what Stella saw in Bobby Lehman, a stocky-built, non-descript sort of guy with a brown flattop haircut that accentuated his receding hairline, hazel eyes and an overblown opinion of his attributes. Tori liked him less now that he was whining, "Oh, God, Stella's not going to marry me," blowing his whiskey breath on the side of her face since she refused to look at him. And she'd liked him even less when Mitch had gotten between Carl and Bobby to stop the brawl and Bobby had inadvertently slugged Mitch in the mouth. If she added the fact that Bobby had stopped Mitch from kissing her in the bar because of his hot head, she would literally despise the pavement he'd crawled upon on his way to the truck.

Now that Mitch had a small split on the left corner of his bottom lip, Tori doubted he'd kiss her tonight. Maybe that wasn't a bad thing. If she wanted him to grant her an interview, she needed to start acting like a professional, not some smitten woman willing to hop into bed with a pedigreed cowboy just because he looked great in jeans, danced like a pro and made her melt with his smile. Besides, she hadn't really wanted to hop into bed with him. She'd wanted to hurl herself into bed with him without a second thought.

"I gotta see my woman," Bobby slurred when they arrived in front of Stella's tiny white frame farmhouse, situated between the edge of town and the verge of nowhere. Tori's accommodations until Sunday.

"That's not a good idea, Bob," Mitch said, bracing an arm across Bobby's chest to hold him back. "You better let her calm down first."

"I'll talk to her," Tori said as she grasped the handle. After she opened the door and slid out of the truck, she smiled at Mitch over Bobby, who was now leaning to one side. "Thanks, Mitch. I guess I'll see you tomorrow night at the wedding."

"If she marries me," Bobby whined again.

Mitch sent Tori a regretful look. "Yeah. Maybe we can finish our *dance*."

His grin, lopsided due to his swollen lip, did things to Tori that she felt all the way to the soles of her feet. "That's a deal."

Just as she reached the gate, Tori heard, "Dammit, Bobby. Get back here!"

Bobby rushed past her, pushing her against the fence as he tore into the house. Stunned, Tori turned to find Mitch rounding the hood, verbalizing the curses she had silently uttered at the drunken groom-to-be.

"He's determined to talk to her," Mitch said when he reached Tori's side.

"I think we both should go in there and referee."

"I think you're probably right."

Tori entered the house with Mitch behind her, finding wobbly Bobby facing off with stern Stella.

"Carl was only congratulating me, you jackass!" Stella shouted, her face stained with tears.

"He had his hand on your back…Stel…" Burp. "…la."

Mitch approached Bobby and grabbed his arm. "Come on, Bob. You need to sleep it off."

Bobby wrenched his arm away and stumbled back against the wall. "I ain't goin' nowhere till she talks to me."

Stella folded her arms beneath her full breasts. "I'm not talking to you right now, Bobby Joe Lehman. I'm not sure I'm even going to marry you."

Without warning, Bobby pushed off the wall and snatched the keys out of Mitch's grasp. "Stella and me are going for a drive."

"No way, Bob," Mitch said. "You're drunk, so give them back."

But before Mitch could snatch them away, Stella grabbed the keys from Bobby, dropped them down her maternity blouse and grinned.

Bobby growled and then went in search of Mitch's keys, running his hands up Stella's blouse like a security guard doing a strip search. Stella squealed and said, "You brute!" but didn't put up one ounce of a fight.

And just like that, Bobby and Stella were kissing and groping like a couple of horny kids, as if all were forgotten, especially that Tori and Mitch were standing there, playing witness to their foreplay.

Tori turned her back on the disgusting scene and told them, "Get a room."

And they did, running hand in hand into the bedroom adjacent to the living room, slamming the door behind them. Tori stared at the closed door, mouth agape and totally shocked into silence.

"Which one of us is going to get my keys?"

Tori turned to Mitch and shook her head. "Not me. Not on your life. You should have put them in your pocket."

"That's the last thing I wanted, Bobby rifling through my pocket." Mitch ran a hand over the back of his neck. "What do you propose I use to get home?"

"Stella's car?"

"You have any idea where she keeps her keys?"

Tori visually searched the room. "In her purse, which is probably in the bedroom with her and Bobby. So I guess you can either call a cab, walk or wait." She really hoped he'd choose the last option.

"No cabs in Quail Run, and no way am I going to walk twenty miles in forty-degree weather." He sauntered over to the floral sofa and set his long, lean body down on the cushions, easy as you please. "I'll wait."

Suddenly very warm, and very thrilled, Tori slipped out of the black leather jacket and hung it on the hook by the opening leading to the kitchen before facing Mitch again. "You know, it could take a while."

"Probably not. Bobby's pretty drunk. I'm not sure he can even get it…" He rubbed his shadowed jaw. "Get anything done."

Tori had no doubt Mitch could get it done, and quite sufficiently, drunk or not. But he wasn't drunk, and neither was Tori, except she felt rather woozy seeing Mitch leaning back on the sofa, his raven hair shining in the light since he'd left his hat in the truck, his long legs stretched out in front of him, his large hands clasped over his board-flat belly, right above the big gleaming silver-and-gold belt buckle, and below that, the big….

Tori forced her gaze back to his eyes. "Bobby's been here the past two nights. From what I've heard, he's rather…determined." So was Tori, determined not to faint over the sheer maleness of Mitch Warner.

"Don't mind me," he said. "You can go on to bed."

Don't mind me? How could she possibly ignore him? "You're sitting on my bed, Mitch."

His grin arrived slowly, bearing down on Tori with the force of an eighteen-wheeler hell-bent for the border. "Oh, yeah? I thought Stella had a spare room."

"She does, but it's full of boxes and furniture ready for the move to the ranch where Bobby works."

"Bobby works for me."

Another shocking revelation. "She didn't tell me that."

"Well, he does." Mitch patted the seat beside him. "Come here. We can talk while Stella and Bob take care of business."

Tori thought it might be better if she suggested they sit at the dinette, not on her makeshift bed, in case she found it difficult to behave. But she was so drawn in by Mitch's diamond-blue gaze that she moved toward the sofa as if he were pulling her forward with an invisible lasso.

She dropped down beside him, keeping a decent berth between them, in case she did forget herself and tackled his fine cowboy bod.

They remained silent for a few moments while Tori worked up the nerve to tell him what she did for a living and then ask him for an official interview. But before she could open her mouth, the trouble commenced, beginning with an "Oh, baby," then an "Oh, Bobby, oh, Bobby, ohhhh...." The thumping against the wall behind the sofa sent both Mitch and Tori off the couch simultaneously.

"Get your jacket and let's get out of here," Mitch said.

Tori complied and met Mitch at the front entrance. "Where are we going?"

"Anywhere but here," he said as he opened the door.

They walked to the truck but when Tori headed for the passenger side, Mitch said, "I locked it."

She faced him again. "No one locks their vehicles in Quail Run."

"I do. I never know when some reporter is going to get it in their head to rummage though my glove box, looking for family secrets."

Tori swallowed hard. Maybe now wasn't a good time to tell him she was a reporter. She'd wait and do it tomorrow night, after the wedding, since she assumed it was still on. The honeymoon obviously was.

On the brink of freezing to the sidewalk, Tori pulled her jacket tighter around her. "Okay, so now what do you suggest we do? Go for a walk?" She nodded toward the closest neighbor's house, which happened to be one pasture over. "We could beg the Wilsons for mercy."

Mitch strode to the back of the truck and pulled the tailgate down. "We can get back here for the time being. I have some hay and a couple of heavy blankets. That'll keep us warm until Stella cries uncle. Or, 'Oh, Bobby!'"

Tori had no doubt that being under a blanket with Mitch Warner would keep her very warm and could get her into serious trouble. But that didn't stop her from saying, "Okay. Guess it's the best we can do for now."

Mitch stepped up into the pickup's bed and held out his hand to help Tori up. Turning his back on her, he crouched down and pulled a wire cutter from the built-in metal toolbox backed up to the cab, snapping the string of wire binding the hay bale while Tori stood on the tailgate and watched.

After scattering some hay and laying a blanket over it, he sat and again patted the spot beside him. "Soft as a feather bed."

As dangerous as one, too, Tori thought. But her teeth were about to chatter right out of her head if she didn't get some heat.

She slipped down beside Mitch where he covered them both with a red-and-black plaid blanket that smelled faintly of hay and oats, their heads propped against the partial bale of hay padding the toolbox. They stared straight ahead, the silence broken only by the occasional gust of wind whistling around them and rustling the leaves in the nearby maple tree. The lone guard light and a sliver of the moon high in the sky provided the only real illumination in the clear, dark night.

"I really can't believe that just happened," Tori said, the heat of her blush offering some relief from the biting cold.

"Me neither. Didn't know old Bobby had it in him."

"Obviously he does since Stella's pregnant."

Tori could feel his gaze lingering over her, caressing her as did his deep, seductive voice when he said, "I wonder if they broke the bed."

"If they haven't by now, it's a pretty sturdy bed."

"So you've had to put up with that every night?"

"Yep, every night. And every time Stella started with the Oh, Bobby, I rolled my eyes and said, 'Oh, brother.'" She turned her head and found he'd turned to his side to face her. "It's absolutely ridiculous, isn't it?"

He smiled, giving the moon and stars some hefty competition. "Which part? The moaning or the fact that they're that passionate about each other?"

Tori rolled to her side, bringing their faces so close she could feel the whisper of his breath against her forehead. "I don't know. Maybe I'm just jealous. My boyfriend never said, Oh, Tori! during…you know."

He frowned. "I thought you didn't have a boyfriend."

"Ex-boyfriend," she corrected. "We broke up a few months ago."

"What went wrong?"

Everything. "He stayed in Oklahoma City when I moved to Dallas. We tried the long-distance relationship for a while, but it didn't last."

"Did you try phone sex?" he asked in an amused tone.

"A guy who considers reading a stock market report as foreplay isn't inclined to having phone sex."

"Yeah, well he must've been a real idiot."

"Honestly, Mike was a nice guy. Just not all that romantic." And not all that easy to love.

"Does that interest you, having someone talking to you during sex?"

Tori shivered at the way Mitch had said the word "sex" as

if he literally knew all the ins and outs. She trembled from the way he studied her with those heavenly blue eyes that made her want to sing a tribute. "I can't really say what I prefer since I haven't had that much experience. I've only had the one boyfriend."

When Mitch pulled the blanket up under their chins, Tori remembered he didn't have on a jacket. "You must be freezing since you're only wearing a shirt."

"Two shirts, and I'm pretty hot-natured."

He was simply hot, Tori decided, and shivered again.

"But you're cold, so let me give you some of my heat," he said in a low, slow-burn voice. He wrapped his arms around her and pulled her closer, doing exactly as he'd promised—giving her his *heat*. And Tori absorbed that heat in some places that were more than adequately covered.

Noting his lip was beginning to swell more, she carefully touched the corner of his mouth above the cut. "You should really make Bobby pay dearly for this."

He surveyed her face for a long moment before his gaze came to rest on her mouth. "Yeah. Bobby owes me for a lot of things, especially for his damn interruption back in the bar."

"No kidding," she said, surprised at how winded she sounded. Even more surprised when Mitch kissed her forehead, her cheek, then rested his oh-so-warm lips against hers.

Tori pulled back. "If we do this, your mouth is going to hurt."

"Not if you kiss it and make it better."

Oh, jeez. Oh, gosh. Oh, my, Tori's final thought when Mitch parted her lips with his tongue, slipping it inside her agreeable mouth.

He tilted his head to avoid touching the slight cut to her lips, but he had no trouble at all kissing her completely, moving his tongue against hers, softly, painstakingly though he didn't appear to be in any pain. Tori was. She ached like the devil from wanting him, knowing that only he could make her particular ache all better.

As the kiss went on and on, deeper and deeper, hotter and hotter, Tori reasoned that the tension that had been building between them in the bar, the sounds of Stella's and Bobby's lovemaking, the sex talk, had added kindling to the campfire. The combination was proving hazardous, threatening to drive them to a possible point of no return. Unless she stopped Mitch, and soon.

But Tori didn't stop him. She didn't want to stop him. Not when he kept kissing her until she thought she'd go up in a blaze of glory. Not when he tugged her sweater up and slipped his hand underneath to cup her breast through black lace. Not when he worked the front closure of her bra, opening it with ease.

She gasped when he contacted her bare flesh.

"I'm sorry my hands are so cold," he murmured in her ear, but kept his callused fingertips working her already rigid nipple.

"Your hands are wonderful," she said, prompting him to kiss her again, this time more deeply, more ardently, more suggestively as he moved his tongue back and forth, imitating the act foremost on her mind.

The next thing Tori knew, she was on her back on the blanket-covered hay and Mitch was partially on top of her, still kneading her breasts with finesse, first one, then the other. She didn't care that they were in a truck bed, not a real bed. She didn't care that it was cold as a well digger's shovel. She didn't care about anything when Mitch lifted her shirt completely, burrowed his way beneath the blanket, and replaced his hand with his lips.

His mouth was definitely hot and so was his tongue that flicked across her nipple before he suckled her with an unyielding tug that made her want to cry, Oh, Mitch!

Tori totally abandoned any arguments against this as she slid her fingers through his silky black hair. She'd never felt so carefree in her life, so totally consumed by a man with a mouth that should be registered as a weapon since it was shooting holes in her common sense.

She was keenly aware of Mitch's erection pressing against

her thigh, the movement of his hips grinding against her, telling her exactly what he needed without saying a word.

Mitch lifted his mouth from her breasts, came up from beneath the blanket and kissed her again, still off-centered but still as effective.

He broke the kiss and whispered, "I want you, Tori, so tell me to stop."

Stop! her mind called out as he worked the button on her pants. Stop! sounded again as he tracked her zipper down. Stop! filtered into her hazy brain as he pushed the leather pants and her panties down her hips to her thighs.

Don't stop! was the voice she chose to heed when he sifted his fingertips through the covering of curls, finding the source of all that need she desperately needed him to satisfy. And he did, with small circular motions, coming nearer and nearer until he hit the mark, causing her hips to rise abruptly from the jolt.

Mitch muttered, "Easy, babe," before kissing her again, not once halting his slow, deliberate ministrations.

"Easy" would describe Tori at the moment and what Mitch probably considered her to be, but again she didn't have the will or wherewithal to stop this, stop him.

She moaned against his mouth when he fondled her with the pad of his thumb and slipped a finger inside her, then another. Such a sweet invasion, such a skilled man, her final grasp on reality before the climax completely took over all reasoning with a pulsating rhythm and sharp, succinct spasms.

But it simply wasn't enough, and wouldn't be until she had all of Mitch. She pulled his denim shirt and T-shirt from his waistband as he had hers, reached up beneath both and glided her palm down the flat plane of his abdomen, over the slight spattering of hair at his navel that thinned when it reached his waistband. It took two hands to loosen the buckle, and two seconds for Mitch to halt the kiss and suck in a deep breath when she released the snap and lowered his fly. He pulled her against his chest and tucked her head beneath his chin. But that didn't prevent her from going forward, going all the way.

He exhaled slowly when she opened his jeans and tugged at his briefs, freeing him. She worked her palms beneath his shirts once more, over the taut terrain of his broad chest, pausing to touch his nipples, then back down, back up again, heating her palms from the friction, sufficiently warming them up so she could do some exploring of her own.

But she didn't have that opportunity since Mitch rose up on his knees, threw back the blanket, pulled her pants and underwear down to her ankles, pushed his jeans and briefs down to his thighs and then pushed inside her before she could draw her next breath.

"Oh, man," Mitch said.

"Oh, wow," she murmured, now totally, completely addicted to the feel of his weight, his tempered thrusts stoking the fire, burning away the last of the cold with his body. Big body…every bit of it.

She ran her palms over his muscled back then down to his buttocks to feel the power as he moved, a little faster and harder each time.

Amazing, Tori thought as he slid his hands beneath her bottom and pulled her fast against him. Incredible was another thought when he whispered sexy words in her ear—words that would send a proper Southern mother for the soap. His breath came in sharp gasps at her ear, hers came in soft puffs as he stroked her with his body and his hand again, and again. Thrust again and again and again…

The second orgasm hit Tori like a tidal wave, knocking her back into oblivion. Mitch's body went rigid in her arms and he stopped moving altogether.

Everything seemed to stop then as Tori shuddered from the impact and Mitch released a long hiss between his teeth, then collapsed against her.

After a time, the stars came back into view, the world started turning again, the cold nipped at her nose and rode out on a fog from her parted lips. But Tori knew that although everything seemed to be back to normal, except for her heartbeat, she would never, ever be the same again. Never.

* * *

This wasn't the first time Mitch Warner had made love to a woman in the bed of a truck, but that had been years ago when no other options had been available. It *was* the first time he'd totally lost control to the point he'd felt like he'd had an out-of-body experience. And the first time that he'd been so tuned into a lover that he'd failed to use a condom.

He thought he should probably move off of Tori, offer some lame excuse for his carelessness, but he didn't have the strength. The cold night air bit at the back of his bare thighs and if he didn't at least cover himself, the tails of his shirt might freeze to his butt. If he didn't roll away from Tori, *they* might freeze this way only to be discovered by the sheriff tomorrow morning, still tangled together, not such an unappealing prospect. But if he didn't get Tori back in the house, he would be tempted to go at it again, not a great idea considering he'd already screwed up once in the protection department, and he hated to think what the consequences might be. Stella and Bob would be the first ones to tell them that unprotected sex leads to unplanned pregnancy.

"I guess this is probably a good time to tell you I've never done this before," Tori said against his shoulder.

Stunned, Mitch raised his head and stared down at her beautiful face. No way would he have not known she was a virgin. Mary Alice had been one all those years ago, but then so had he. He sure as hell wasn't a novice now. He would have known. "I thought you said that you and your boyfriend—"

"I meant I've never had sex with someone I've just met. Ever."

Mitch couldn't lay claim to that, but for the past decade, he'd settled for convenience and comfort with Mary Alice instead of hot, unrestrained sex with a virtual stranger—hot unprotected sex—until tonight. Until Tori.

Finally, he rolled away from her onto his back, reached down and pulled the blanket back into place, not only to keep her warm but also to keep the temptation to make love to her again corralled.

After they pulled their clothes back into place, redid and re-snapped, they resumed their original positions staring at the sky, not touching, not speaking, until Mitch couldn't stand it any longer. He had to know exactly how dire their situation might be.

"Tori, are you on the Pill?"

"Kind of late to be asking me that, Mitch."

No kidding. "I know."

"The answer is no."

Oh, hell. "Then—"

"But I have taken a birth control shot, so we should be okay. At least where pregnancy is concerned. I know I'm safe in the disease department. I've only been with one man."

"So am I. I've only been with one woman for the past nine years."

"Mary Alice."

He glanced at her but she continued to study the stars. "How did you know about that?"

"This is a small town, Mitch. People talk. That's why you have to promise me you won't say anything about this."

The concern in her voice led to his reassurance. "I'm not going to tell anyone, Tori. You can trust me."

"Good. I wouldn't want anyone to think that I'm…."

When her voice trailed off, Mitch turned to his side again and pulled her over to face him. "Wouldn't want anyone to think that you're what?"

"You know. Someone who would do this kind of thing." She released a humorless laugh. "That's really stupid considering I did do this, and we are consenting adults, and it's really no one's business—"

Mitch stopped her words with a kiss then bracketed her face in his palms. "I don't think any less of you, Tori. It's just one of those things that happens when two people are attracted to each other."

She laid a dramatic hand on her chest and grinned, though Mitch still saw the worry in her dark eyes. "Does this mean you still like me?"

Mitch laughed, something he didn't do that often, especially not in the presence of a woman. "Yeah, Tori, I like you." And he did, a lot.

"Okay, that's great. But if you really like me, then you'll find a way to get your keys before we both turn into human icicles."

Mitch started to protest, to ask her to put her incredible body back against his so they could have a little more time together, something that was damn out of character for him. He normally wasn't the let's-hold-each-other-after-sex kind of guy, but then this wasn't exactly a normal situation. And Tori wasn't just any woman. But he also realized that they both needed some sleep so they wouldn't pass out during the wedding tomorrow night.

Tomorrow night. Maybe they could have a repeat performance, out of the elements and in a real bed. His bed. And he wouldn't be so careless the next time.

That alone spurred Mitch from beneath the covers and onto his feet to hold out his hand and help Tori up. Once they were standing, he took the opportunity to pull her against his chest one more time, feel her against him one more time, kiss her one more time before letting her go.

After they left the truck, they walked the path in silence and stopped at the front door, where they found the pilfered keys taped to the screen.

Mitch yanked them down and tossed them up, snatching them in midair. "At least I didn't have to go frisk Stella to find these. That would have really sent Bobby over the edge."

Tori's smile was soft and self-conscious. "I'm sure Bobby's out like a light. At least I hope so."

They stared at each other for a solid few seconds before Mitch leaned over and this time kissed her cheek, fearing if he did more he'd be tempted to ask her if he could join her on the sofa.

"I had a good time tonight, Tori." A serious understatement. He'd had a great time. The best time he'd had in a long, long time.

"So did I." She rubbed her hands down her arms. "But I think it's probably wise if we don't have quite as good a time tomorrow night."

So much for his plans. "You're probably right." And she probably was, but Mitch couldn't help hoping that maybe he might have more of what he'd experienced with her tonight, just one last time before she left. But he wouldn't ask that of her, not now. Not when he could see the guilt calling out from her dark eyes.

"Tell Bobby I'll be by to get him in the morning since it's bad luck to see the bride on the day of the wedding."

"Okay, but it's too late for that. He's going to see her unless I blindfold him."

"Probably not a bad idea at that. He's going to have one hell of a headache and the sun isn't going to help."

"Serves him right." Tori sent him another smile as she opened the screen. "Guess I'll see you at the altar."

Mitch experienced a sharp stab of fear. "At the altar?"

She frowned. "Stella and Bobby's wedding?"

Damn. He was acting like a total fool. "Yeah. The wedding. Stella and Bob's wedding at Stella's parents' house. Tomorrow night."

When she opened the door, he said, "One more thing."

She faced him again, her long, slender fingers curled around the handle. "What?"

"I just want you to know that I'm not normally this careless."

"Me neither. Guess we were just feeling a little frisky."

When she smiled again, he wanted to kiss her again. Real bad. "'Night Tori."

"Good night, Mitch."

He watched her slip inside the house and close the door, then watched the door some more, hoping she might come back out. Hoping she might invite him in. Like that was going to happen. He'd totally screwed up everything by doing something he should never have done. Something he hoped wouldn't affect both his and Tori's future. But he had to trust that what she'd said was true—she couldn't get pregnant.

Shoving his hands into his pockets, Mitch walked back to the truck and slid inside, calling himself ten kinds of a fool for losing control, vowing to forget this ever happened. But when he started the engine and turned on the heat full blast, he could smell Tori's floral scent flowing through the truck—a scent that was all over his clothes, all over his body.

The taste of her was still fresh in his mind, on his tongue, jump-starting his desire back to life when he recalled in great detail how it had felt to be inside her. How he had totally, completely lost himself in the moment. And just as important, how it had felt to talk to a woman who'd actually listened to what he'd said, a woman who'd treated him like a man, not like a means to maintain her status among Quail Run's limited elite—like Mary Alice Marshall, who'd recently turned her affections to Brady Stevens, the banker. More like to his checkbook.

Mitch really didn't care. The relationship had been going nowhere for years, and they'd both realized that for a while now. In fact, he'd been relieved when Mary Alice had called it off. He was really glad she had, especially tonight. Otherwise, he might still be settling for convenience, missing out on making love with an angel. An experience he wouldn't soon forget.

Regardless, he would try to avoid repeating the reckless behavior tomorrow night, even if he couldn't avoid Tori. He would be a gentleman and keep his hands to himself, if that was what she wanted.

But he wasn't going to like it. Not one damn bit.

Tori leaned against the closed door with eyes shut tight. Even though it was warm inside the house, she felt chilled to the marrow.

"Where have you been, Victoria May?"

Her eyes snapped open to find Stella seated on the frayed tan chair wearing a tattered robe, her hair in curlers and her eyes blurry with sleep. "Why are you still awake?"

"Bobby's snoring like a freight train."

Tori pushed away from the door. "What? No, 'Give it to me Stella?'"

Stella blushed like a vine-ripe tomato. "You heard that?"

"I heard plenty. So did Mitch. That's why we left." Tori re-hung her coat back on the rack and started toward the small hall that led to the bathroom. "I'm going to take a shower." And try to wash away the remnants of the mistake she'd just made.

Stella stood and blocked the path. "You didn't answer my question. Where did you and Mitch go?"

"We sat in the back of his truck."

"What did you do back there?"

"Uh, we talked."

"Only talked?"

Tori didn't dare tell Stella anything different and not because she didn't trust her. She just didn't want to have to explain her imprudent behavior. "Yeah. We talked. General conversation. You and Bobby ought to try it."

Stella grinned and yanked a piece of straw from Tori's hair, holding it up as if she'd found the prize egg at Easter. "Looks to me like someone had a roll in the hay."

Tori strode to the sofa, perched on the edge and covered her face in her hands to hide the guilt. "We did it," she blurted out, then peeked between her fingers to see Stella's reaction.

Stella hovered over her with eyes as wide as world globes. "You mean you 'did it' as in made love with Mitch Warner?"

Tori dropped her hands to her lap and fell back against the sofa. "We had sex, Stella. You can't make love with someone you barely know."

Stella took a seat beside her. "Was it great?"

Tori could feel the flames rise to her face. "Oh, yeah. Better than great."

Stella slapped Tori hard on the thigh. "It's about time you took a few chances."

Unfortunately, Tori had taken a huge chance that she wished she could take back. "We didn't use anything for protection."

Tori didn't think Stella's eyes could get any wider, but they did. "Oh, no. Don't you know what can happen when you do that?"

Oh, yes, Tori knew exactly what could happen because it had happened to her mother and to Stella. She'd been certain that she was above such carelessness. A fine time to have a common sense lapse.

"Do you think you might be pregnant?" Stella asked.

"I'm hoping I'm not. I took a shot a while ago."

"Define 'a while.'"

"About five months ago."

"Isn't that a little long for it to still be of use, Tori?"

"Yes, although sometimes it takes women up to a year to get pregnant. I just didn't have any reason to get another one after Mike and I broke up." Until tonight.

"If you are pregnant, what are you going to do?"

Have a baby, Tori decided. Her mother had done it without a husband; she could do it, too. But hopefully it wouldn't have to come to that.

Tori came to her feet and headed toward the bathroom. "I'm not going to worry about it now. I'd just be borrowing trouble."

And if she let things get out of hand with Mitch again, she'd be borrowing a national debt's worth of trouble. She still wanted the interview, but she doubted she would have the nerve to ask. She wasn't sure she could even face him again.

But she had to face him tomorrow night at the wedding. Beyond that, she would just take it one step at a time—and hope that she didn't find herself repeating her mother's history and stepping into his arms because she just couldn't resist him.

She had to resist him. She also had to consider that she still had an opportunity she couldn't pass up. But if she didn't get him to agree to giving her a story, she would be leaving on Sunday. Leaving him and this intolerant town behind. And hopefully she wouldn't be leaving with a little reminder of the night she'd found sheer heaven in a maverick cowboy's strong arms.

Three

The following evening, Tori stood in her best friend's bedroom where she'd spent many a day during her youth, giggling over boys and even crying over them a time or two. The house had been her haven, her home away from home. The place where she'd felt welcome, never judged or pitied. She had known unconditional love and acceptance from Stella's parents, who now waited downstairs to witness the marriage of their only daughter. Tori would never know the pleasure of having her mom in attendance should she decide to wed, and that made her sad on a night that should be filled with joy.

The soft sounds of taped music signaled the ceremony was about to take place in the Moores' living room among select family and friends. Mitch was downstairs, too, and that created havoc on Tori's heartbeat, more than the prospect of singing in front of a whole slew of people. She'd hidden out that morning when he'd come to retrieve Bobby, and he'd nixed the brief rehearsal right before noon due to ranch obligations, sending his apologies and assurances to Stella that he knew what to do.

Tori couldn't argue that one bit. Last night, he'd known exactly what he was doing.

At least she wouldn't have to talk to him during the service. Of course, she couldn't very well avoid him at the reception without looking obvious. Exactly what did one say to someone following one reckless night? She didn't have a clue, nor could she afford to think about that now.

Smoothing a hand over the long-sleeve, tea-length red velvet dress, Tori hoped she hadn't left a spot from her perspiring palms. Stella sat at the dressing table while Janie and Brianne applied the finishing touches on her makeup. All of them had been uncharacteristically quiet in light of the event—the first of the "Fearsome Foursome" was about to embark on matrimony and parenthood.

Tori wondered if in a few short years they would all be soccer moms. Not her, she decided. She wanted to make a solid go of her career before she even considered settling into a normal routine. She also wanted a two-parent home, something she hadn't had. She could not in good conscience subject her child to that kind of existence, even though she'd done okay. She wanted more than okay. She wanted it all—the career, the home, the husband and the kids. All in good time, unless….

Her interlude with Mitch Warner once again weaseled its way into her mind. Carelessness, plain and simple, and hopefully without repercussions.

The bouquet of red roses and stephanotis began to shake in Tori's hand when she recalled their lovemaking. How was she going to face him if she couldn't maintain a good grip on a bunch of posies?

"Okay, we're ready," Brianne proclaimed, drawing Tori's attention.

Stella was standing now, the fingertip-length veil somewhat concealing her face but the plain lace sheath couldn't conceal her pregnancy. However, the dress was tasteful—and white—something that would have been unheard of a decade ago, especially in this hypercritical town. Maybe things had changed. Or maybe Stella just didn't care what everyone else thought.

"You look beautiful, Stella," Tori said sincerely, her voice shaky as she fought back sentimental tears. "Bobby is going to be so proud of you."

Stella frowned, although her eyes misted. "Bobby's lucky I'm still marrying him."

"And he's very lucky to have you," Brianne said as she swiped a hand over the moisture on her own cheeks.

Janie walked to the door and opened it wide. "Okay, let's go before we all start blubbering and ruin our makeup. Single file. I'm first, then Brianne, then Tori. Stella, you're bringing up the rear."

Brianne blew out a frustrated breath. "We know, Janie. We've already been through the routine."

Janie shot an acrimonious look over one shoulder. "I just want to make sure we have it straight."

Tori couldn't hide her smile over Janie's assertiveness and need to organize. Some things never changed, at least inwardly. She patted Stella's arm and said, "Break a leg, kiddo," before moving in front of her.

"Not a nice thing to say to a pregnant bride who's expected to walk down a flight of stairs in heels," Stella muttered from behind her.

The sound of the *Wedding March* filtered in from the parlor below. Janie sent them all a "thumbs-up" then began her descent. As earlier rehearsed, Tori waited until Brianne had taken three steps then started down the stairs behind her.

The makeshift aisle was flanked by four rows of white chairs on either side, all filled to capacity. Some guests lined the walls and although the living room was larger than most, the masses made the room seem to close in on Tori. Anticipation and adrenaline sent her pulse on a sprint as she continued her descent.

When she reached the red runner covering the carpet, Tori scanned the front of the room, namely the groomsmen. With his sandy stylish hair and charmer's smile, Clint Moore looked handsome as always, even if he was a playboy extraordinaire. Bobby's older brother, Johnny, bald as a bowling ball and grinning like a madman, stood at Clint's right. And on his left, nearest the groom, one man literally stood above the crowd.

Dressed in a standard black tuxedo, Mitch Warner had morphed into the senator's son, his boots the only indication that he preferred prime cattle to a political caucus. His eyes were as blue as his blood, his hair as black as the dark before the dawn, a perfect masculine package that could be marketed as Every Woman's Fantasy.

In that moment, Tori felt about as "country bumpkin" and nondescript as she'd ever felt in her life. Mitch was luminous and charismatic, especially his smile that he now aimed on her. A smile that could wilt her bouquet.

Tori's steps faltered for an instant. If she didn't watch it, she'd take a misstep, end up posterior over pride in the aisle and be forced to sing "Send in the Clowns" instead of "The Wedding Song." Of course, if Bobby had had his way, she'd be belting out "I've Got Friends in Low Places." Lucky for her, and the esteemed guests, Stella's good taste had won out.

After she took her position before the red brick fireplace where the pastor, Janie and Brianne now stood, Tori turned to watch Stella gliding down the aisle on her father's arm, glowing like a summer firefly. Tori hoped that she would be so happy when her time finally came, *if* her time finally came.

Stella reached the front of the aisle, accepted a kiss from her dad, then joined hands with Bobby. The intro of the song began and for a minute, Tori thought she might miss her cue when her traitorous gaze landed on Mitch. But instinct took over and she sang the lyrics without fail, focusing on a framed family portrait across the room to avoid looking at the guests, particularly the best man.

When she'd ended the song, the minister began the simple ceremony. Stella's voice trembled as she repeated her vows, yet she said them without hesitation. Bobby sounded a little shaken up, but he didn't waver with the "I dos" either. Tori didn't dare venture another glance in Mitch's direction when Bobby engaged Stella in a rather lengthy kiss. But she couldn't avoid him when the service ended and he joined her for the trek back down the aisle behind the happy couple.

Gosh, he smelled great, Tori thought as she rested her hand in the bend of his arm. He murmured something but she couldn't quite hear him due to the resounding applause. As it turned out, Mitch's words would remain a mystery, since the wedding party was quickly ushered into separate limousines brought all the way from Oklahoma City for the reception—the bridesmaids in one car, the groomsmen in the other. Bobby and Stella climbed into Bobby's truck, now sporting a lengthy string of beer cans, inflated condoms tied to the antennae and She Got Him Today, He'll Get Her Tonight emblazoned in white letters across the closed tailgate.

"Classy," Tori muttered as they traveled the mile to Sadler's that had been reserved for the private reception. "I've never understood why men get such a kick out of writing dirty sayings on the wedding vehicle."

Janie sighed. "I've never understood why Stella chose Bobby, but she's stuck with him now."

"She's in love," Brianne said. "And we're all just jealous."

Tori remained silent even though she secretly acknowledged that in some ways Brianne was right. Human nature dictated a need to be loved. She was no different.

After they arrived, Tori trailed her friends into the club, her heart doing a jig when she considered Mitch was probably already inside. Her assumptions were confirmed when she glimpsed him standing near the beer keg talking to a leggy blonde with a neat upsweep and a neck as slender as a swan's. Her strapless dress revealed abundant breasts that looked as if they might launch from the bodice if she raised her arms even a tad. Her lips were unnaturally full and her diamond-encrusted hand kept landing on Mitch's arm. It wasn't until she glanced her way that Tori recognized the woman—Mary Alice Marshall.

Stung by an utterly ridiculous prick of jealousy, Tori wandered away from the disconcerting sight to stand in line with the guests waiting to congratulate the bride and groom, while Clint kept Janie and Brianne entertained near the bar with Lord only knew what kind of stories. But she couldn't keep her eyes off the harlot and Mitch still involved in a conversation. And by the way, wasn't Miss Mary Alice engaged? Tori wondered exactly where the fiancé might be. Maybe he hadn't been invited. She seriously doubted that. She did not doubt that Mary A. still had designs on Mitch, apparent by the way the woman kept moving closer to him, touching him with a familiarity shared by longtime lovers. Lovers who were still lovers.

Tori experienced a sense of satisfaction when Mitch began tugging at his bow tie and glancing around the room. After he frowned and pointed toward Stella and Bobby, Mary Alice left his side with a flip of her wrist and swayed away, tossing a suggestive look and steamy smile over one shoulder.

In order not to look too interested in Mitch's whereabouts, Tori studied the groom's cake as she waited for the crowd surrounding the honored couple to dissipate. Leave it to Bobby to request a plastic pickup truck and toy horses as decoration. But then, Mitch might prefer something similar at his wedding. Boy, wouldn't he make a terrific-looking groom? And she wouldn't mind being his bride.

Heavens, where did that thought come from? She needed to quit thinking about him on those terms. After all, they'd spent only one night together in the bed of a truck. Pure and simple lust, spontaneous sex. That's all it had been, and she didn't plan on an encore. She had to start considering how she would ask him for the interview, now that she gathered he was still speaking to her. But how long would that hold true once he learned she was a member of the hated media?

She'd give it her best shot at explaining why she hadn't told him sooner, ask for the story and, if not successful, return home tomorrow and forget everything that had happened between them...in a year or two.

The tap on her shoulder startled her, stealing her breath when she considered that maybe Mitch was standing behind her. Even though her heart was running at sprinter speed, she retained enough composure to turn slowly instead of spinning around like a frenzied top. Disappointment, then surprise, overtook her when she realized Mary Alice Marshall, not Mitch, had taken her place in the dwindling receiving line.

"Do I know you?" she asked, her tone just a little too sweet for Tori's taste.

"I graduated from Quail Run High three years after you."

Mary Alice tapped a perfect pink nail against her chin. "Oh, that's right. You're that really smart poor girl."

And you were that stuck-up, cheerleader hussy. "True, I was valedictorian."

"How nice. Why are you back?"

Sheesh. Wasn't that obvious? Tori decided Miss Mary Alice probably didn't make it into the top seventy-five percent of her class of twenty-five. "I'm Stella's maid of honor."

The light came on in Mary Alice's expression. Dim, but still on. "Oh, of course." She made a sweeping gesture toward Tori's gown. "That's the reason for the, um, dress. You know, velvet would not have been my choice."

Tori graciously chose to ignore the dig at Stella's taste. "I didn't see you at the wedding."

"That's because Brady and I didn't go to the wedding. We had a prior commitment."

Probably engaged in riveting conversation about the new hardware store the bank had financed, Tori decided. "Ah, yes. Brady, your fiancé."

Mary Alice wrinkled her nose. "How did you know about him?"

She pointed at the comet-sized diamond on Mary Alice's left hand. "Well, that's a dead giveaway. And people are fairly free with the latest gossip."

"True. The news of mine and Brady's engagement has been the talk of the town."

A prime example of a definite lack of excitement in Dullsville. "So when's the big day, Mary Alice?"

"Oh, not until next summer. Brady's building us a new house. Four-thousand square feet on Hunter's Hill." She nodded toward two men conversing in the corner. "That's my sweetie over there, talking to Daddy. He's absolutely wonderful. He will do anything I ask of him."

Anything that involved money, no doubt, because Tori couldn't imagine, or didn't want to imagine, Mary Alice having randy sex with Brady Stevens.

Tori smiled and raked her brain to try and think of something complimentary to say about the town's banker. That was a tough one considering he was at least two inches shorter than Mary Alice, suffered from the beginnings of male pattern baldness and wore the most ill-fitting green suit Tori had ever seen. She found it hard to believe that Mary Alice Marshall had traded in Mitch for a milquetoast. Or maybe Mitch had traded her in. She couldn't imagine what Mitch had seen in her. Actually, she could imagine. It probably involved her bra size, not her brain.

Enough with the nastiness, Victoria.

She gave Mary Alice a benevolent smile. "I'm sure he's great." And rich.

"He is. He's going to make a fine husband." Mary Alice presented an artificial grin. If she were any more transparent, she'd be invisible. "How long will you be staying? Maybe we could do lunch."

Oh, yeah. Down at the local barbecue joint gnawing on messy ribs with the local debutante. What a nice way to spend a day. "That depends. I could be leaving tomorrow or hanging around for a week or so."

"And what will determine that?"

Tori didn't dare go there, although it was tempting to tell Miss Mary Alice she might be spending her days with the former boyfriend. "If Stella and Bobby need my help settling in, I'll be here a little longer."

"Then you'd be staying out at the Independence Ranch?"

Tori simply couldn't resist getting a rise out of the woman.

"I haven't talked to Mitch about it yet, but I'm sure I'd be more than welcome there."

The smile dropped from Mary Alice's overly painted lips. "You've met Mitch?"

"We met last night at Sadler's. He's been very accommodating." If Mary Alice knew exactly how accommodating, she'd probably fall over in her fake designer heels. "He's a very nice man."

"Yes, he is, if you like that cowboy sort. Frankly, I prefer someone more refined."

As Tori suspected, Mitch had dumped the deb. "Like Brady?"

"Yes, and that reminds me. I should join him now. I'm sure he's wondering where I am."

Tori glanced to her right to find Brady chatting with a roving waitress, not looking at all concerned. She hid her smile when she turned her attention to Mary Alice. "Aren't you going to congratulate the bride and groom?"

"Actually, no. I don't know Stella all that well and I've never cared much for Bobby. I just think it's so sad they had to get married."

Tori saw red, and it wasn't the beer sign in the corner. "Bobby and Stella love each other very much."

Mary Alice flipped her ring-bedecked hand in a dismissive gesture. "I'm sure they do. They're perfect for each other. Down home without a pot to pee in. I hear they can't even afford a real honeymoon."

Tori had the sudden urge to kick off her heels, hike up her dress and take Mary Alice down to the ground for a good hair-pulling cat fight. She'd never done that before, but then she'd never done what she'd done last night, either. Neither would qualify as classy, so she chose to verbally sink in her claws. "Stella and Bobby chose not to go on their honeymoon right away because Mitch needs him on the ranch for now. And speaking of Mitch, I think I'll go find him and ask him if he has room for me. You have a nice night with Brady."

Mary Alice's eyes narrowed into a menacing glare. "Oh, I'm sure Mitch has room for you out in the bunkhouse. He's always kind to the common folk."

With that, she pivoted and headed away, leaving Tori clamoring for some scathing comeback. But wasting energy on the likes of Mary Alice Marshall was futile. She had learned that at a very early age.

Finally, Bobby and Stella were alone, holding each other in a death grip and acting as if no one else existed. Tori hated to interrupt, but she wanted to congratulate them one more time before she grabbed some champagne to bolster her courage before she sought out the senator's son.

When she approached, Stella held out her hand and they hugged each other for a long time. Tori pulled away first and said, "Guess you're an old married woman now."

Stella held up her left hand that now sported a plain white gold band. "Yep, and one of these days, I expect to serve as your maid of honor, as long as you don't make me sing."

Bobby sent Tori a comical grin. "That would clear a room real fast."

Stella smacked him on the arm. "We've been married less than hour, and already you're in trouble." She turned back to Tori. "Speaking of singing, you did a beautiful job."

"She looked damn beautiful doing it, too."

Tori went into freeze mode at the sound of the voice behind her. A deep, provocative voice that generated enough heat to thaw her quickly.

She faced Mitch and murmured, "Thank you."

"So here we are again," he said when Stella and Bobby turned their attentions back to each other.

Obviously, the feline Tori had momentarily become in Mary Alice's presence had its claws in her tongue. Or maybe it was Mitch's smile, his face, his hair, his tuxedo or any myriad aspect of the man that kept her momentarily mute.

"You look nice tonight," she finally managed. "Very debonair. And your lip is barely swollen."

"And you look great in that dress. I told you that when we were walking down the aisle."

Mystery solved. "I guess I didn't hear you. But thanks again."

"I'm also wondering what you have on underneath it."

Tori had definitely heard that, loud and clear. But that was the last thing she heard, because the hired band picked that moment to begin a lively number, making normal conversation impossible, which became evident when Mitch said something else that Tori couldn't begin to understand. "What?" she practically shouted.

He leaned closer to her ear, his warm breath trailing over her jaw. "We need to talk. Alone."

Exactly what Tori had been thinking all night. "Okay. I have something I need to ask you, too. After Stella and Bobby cut the cake. "

Mitch nodded toward the dance floor now containing the bride and groom melded together, cheek to cheek. "That could be a while. I suggest we talk in the meantime."

Tori looked around. "Where?"

"Outside. In the truck."

"Are you sure that's a good idea?"

He gave her a knock-me-out grin. "Inside the truck this time."

This time. A vision of another bout of lovemaking in the cab of Mitch's truck attacked her.

No! No! No!

She could not go there again, even if she dearly wanted to take that trip. This encounter would be about business, and she hoped that after she made her proposal, he wouldn't boot her out of the truck onto her behind. "Okay. But I need to be back soon."

"No problem."

Mitch gestured toward the door and on the way out, picked up two champagne glasses, stuck one in each pocket, and then grabbed an open bottle of bubbly from the startled bartender.

Tori followed Mitch out the door, thinking his charisma mixed with cheap champagne could prove to be a fatal combination. She would only have a small glass, just enough to give her a little bravado.

Once they were settled in the truck—Mitch behind the wheel and Tori crouched in the corner of the cab—he turned on the ignition.

"Are we going somewhere?" she asked.

"No. I just want to turn on the heat before you freeze to death."

Although the temperature was somewhat milder tonight, Tori still shivered when a draft of air from the blower hit her full force.

"It should warm up in a minute," Mitch said as he poured the champagne.

Tori was already heating up from his presence alone. Just watching his hands in action turned her on. Ignoring him would be a lost cause.

After he was finished, he situated the bottle between his thighs, drawing Tori's gaze to the male terrain much more obscure in dress slacks than in jeans. But she remembered how those thighs had felt against hers, the tickle of masculine hair, the tensile muscles, the absolute power.

"Tori, do you want some of this?"

Oh, yeah.

Mortified, Tori tore her gaze from his lap and focused on his chin. Darn him, he didn't even try to hide the fact that he knew what she'd been thinking. That knowledge was etched all over his gorgeous face, sparkling in his eyes, present in his smile that sent the mercury rising in her body despite the chilly interior.

She took the glass he offered and a quick drink of champagne. The bubbles tickled her tongue, but not as strongly as Mitch Warner tickled her feminine fancy.

He held up his glass and said, "To the happy couple. Thank God they actually went through with it."

Tori tipped her glass to his. "Amen."

They sipped in silence until Mitch grimaced and said, "You know, I've hated this stuff since my first glass at sixteen. I've only had it once more in the past ten years."

"Another celebration?"

"The day I graduated from Harvard."

A reminder of exactly who he was and why Tori needed to tell him who she was. First, she would concentrate on congenial conversation. "I would have taken you for a beer drinker."

"I am. But the Warner household didn't serve something as lowly as beer, unless it was a high-dollar import."

The venom in his tone took Tori aback. Obviously he did have somewhat of a temper. She gulped another quick drink, keeping her distance in order to thwart the temptation to smooth the tightness from his clean-shaven jaw.

"I guess I should say I'm sorry about last night," he said after a bout of silence. "But I'm not sorry it happened."

Neither was Tori. "I really can't believe we did it in the bed of a truck."

"All things considered, it was still great."

"Was it?"

His gaze zipped to hers. "You didn't think so?"

She chewed her bottom lip. "I guess on a scale from one to ten, I'd give it an eight." In reality, she'd give it a twenty.

He set his champagne on the dash, tipped his head back against the seat and streaked both hands through his hair. "Only an eight?"

"Well, considering it was rather frigid—"

"I don't think anyone qualified as frigid."

"You know what I mean. We didn't really get undressed, understandably so."

"I thought we did pretty well improvising."

"You could say that."

He lifted his head and aimed his intense blue eyes on her. "I could also say that I didn't notice the cold at all because, lady, you were pretty damned hot last night."

Oh, Lordy. Hot behavior was not normally her forte. But then, Mitch Warner was pretty darned hot himself. She'd spent her life learning to compose words to fit the situation, describe the mood, in this case, the man. "Powerful," came to mind. A sensual, magnetic field. A lean, mean love machine. Not enough adjectives of praise existed to do him justice.

Tori stared at her glass instead of him. "If you say so."

He reached over and tipped her chin up with his thumb, forcing her to look at him again. "I definitely say so." He ran one fingertip over her jaw then down her neck. "And I want to apologize again for being so careless."

"We really don't have to go there, Mitch."

His toxic blue eyes melted her from the inside out. "I want to go there again, Tori. With you. All night."

Before Tori had a chance to prepare, he leaned over and slid his tongue across the seam of her lips. "Champagne tastes pretty damn good on you."

"Mitch, I don't think—"

"Don't think, Tori." He took her glass and placed it next to his on the dash, then shoved the open bottle between his seat and the door. "Thinking is overrated."

Tori was overheated, on the brink of incineration when he took her into his arms and kissed her deeply. The tart taste of wine lingered on his tongue, his slow, steady thrusts displaying his need that matched her own. In spite of her previous goal, she couldn't garner the strength to stop him. Couldn't even consider anything but the softness of his tempting lips, the scent of his tantalizing cologne, the glide of his talented hand over her hip as he pulled her closer.

Breaking the kiss, he murmured, "This velvet feels great."

So did his mouth on her neck, hot and damp as he graced it with soft kisses, working his way to her ear. "I want to take this dress off of you. Then I want to rub it all over your body. And mine."

Tori wanted that too. Boy, did she want that.

And she just might get it, she decided, when he reached for

the back zipper and slid it down. "You mean take it off here? Now?" Her voice sounded unnaturally tinny and shrill.

"Not completely," he whispered. "Only a little. I just want to touch you a little. Then I want to take you to my bed where we can do this right. I want to see you naked." His voice sounded smooth, but his breathing sounded shallow. So was Tori's, what little breath she had left.

Tori lost all her will, all her logic, when he slipped the dress off her right shoulder, exposing the top of her bra. She clung to his head, threading her fingers through his thick, dark hair while he brushed kisses across the rise of her breast, using his tongue to make tempting incursions beneath the red lace. Slowly he inched the fabric down until he revealed her nipple for the wicked workings of his lips. The steady pull of his mouth hurtled heat straight to her thighs where his hand now worked the dress upward. In a matter of minutes, she would completely forget why she'd agreed to this rendezvous if she didn't put an end to this now.

Framing his jaws in her palms, she pulled his head up and gave him a beseeching look. "Mitch, we have to stop before we can't."

He straightened and sighed. "I know."

After redoing her dress, he scooted over to his side of the truck and tipped his forehead against the steering wheel. "You're going to be hard-pressed to believe this, but I don't normally come on that strong. It's you. You make me crazy."

Tori couldn't recall when a man had ever said that to her, but she couldn't let flattery or his sensuality rule her head. And she wondered how crazy he would be once she told him the truth.

He lifted his head and glanced her way again. "Now, what did you want to ask me? Let's make it quick so we can get out of here, get on with the festivities, then get on with some more pleasurable activities."

Damn his confidence. She hadn't even said she was willing to go to bed with him again, even though, if things were different, she certainly would.

The man was sufficiently sucking her mind as dry as an Oklahoma gulch in late summer. For that reason, she focused on the two barely touched glasses of champagne sitting side by side on the dash. "Actually, I have a request. But first, I need to tell you something."

"You have a boyfriend."

"No, that's not it."

"Husband?"

"I'm serious, Mitch."

"I can tell. So if you don't have another lover, what is it?"

"I need something from you." And that sounded totally questionable to Tori. She could only imagine how it had sounded to him.

She knew exactly how it had sounded when he said, "I've already told you I'm ready to give you whatever you need, all night long, this time in a real bed."

Oh, how tempting it would be to tell him to take her away and make good on that promise. But she couldn't. "I'm not referring to sex."

His sigh sounded highly frustrated. "Okay, Tori, you're confusing the hell out of me here. Just spit it out."

She drew in a long breath and released it slowly. "I'm a journalist, and I want your story."

Four

This was the closest Mitch had ever come to being sucker punched by a woman. He sat silent for a few moments to let the revelation sink in. Shock gave way to anger and the bitter taste of betrayal overrode the sweet taste of Tori still lingering on his lips.

He risked a look to find her studying her joined hands. "Why the hell didn't you tell me this last night?"

She lifted one shoulder in a shrug, the same shoulder he'd kissed only moments before. "I was going to say something when we were at Stella's, but when you made the comment about the press rifling in your glove box, I just lost my nerve. Later, I, uh, had other things on mind."

She'd had her hands all over his body. He didn't need to remember how great last night had been, or how much he had hoped for a repeat performance tonight. He needed to hang on to his anger. For all intents and purposes, she was the enemy.

"I'm not your enemy, Mitch," she said as if she'd read his mind.

"I've never found one friend among the media."

"Not every journalist buys into sensationalism. Some of us are responsible."

He shot her a hard look. "I have a difficult time believing that, especially since you didn't bother to let me in on your little secret."

She touched his arm then drew back, like she'd forgotten herself. "If you'll just listen for a minute, I'll explain why I think it will be to your advantage to let me do an interview."

Under normal circumstances, Mitch would admire her persistence. But nothing about their relationship so far had been even remotely normal. Not their initial meeting. Not their sexual beginning. Not his undeniable attraction to her that still lived on even after what he now knew. "There's nothing advantageous about spilling your guts. I value my privacy. I've worked damn hard to escape the attention. No need to stir it up again."

"It's going to get stirred up since your father's probably about to announce his retirement."

"I don't give a damn about politics."

"Then you might consider stating your position now rather than let the speculation start to fly. Define your aspirations before someone does it for you. I'm willing to help you."

He ran a hand over his face and stared straight ahead. Some of what she'd said made sense, but he wasn't into logic right now. "You have no idea what it's like to have every detail of your life exposed so everyone can take a jab."

"Actually, I do."

The hint of pain in her voice brought Mitch's attention back to her. "How so?"

"It doesn't matter."

It did to him, even though it probably shouldn't. "Hey, if you expect me to open up to you, it's only fair you do the same."

"This isn't about me. This is about an opportunity you shouldn't pass up."

"I don't want my life plastered all over some newspaper."

"It's not a newspaper. I work for a Dallas women's magazine. We feature stories about successful men in Texas."

"I don't live in Texas, in case you haven't noticed." He couldn't control his sarcasm, yet it didn't seem to dissuade Tori.

"But you're from a prominent Texas political dynasty, so that counts. I'm proposing a story that focuses on your life as a rancher, not as a politician's son. If you don't intend to follow in your father's footsteps, then this is the perfect venue to let that be known."

"And what's in it for you?"

"Well, honestly, it would mean more visibility for me. Possibly a promotion."

The anger came back with the realization he'd been set up by a woman who'd incited his total loss of control and moved him more than any woman he had known. "You had this planned the minute you stepped into town, didn't you? Pretty damned convenient to have Stella and Bob's wedding as a front."

She looked on the verge of getting mad, and he wanted her that way. He wanted her as mad as he was at the moment. Mad over the deception. Mad because this wasn't the way tonight was supposed to end. "For your information," she said, "it didn't occur to me to ask for the interview until you stepped into the bar last night."

Irrational anger overwhelmed his usual common sense. "So was that what our little interlude was all about, sex for a story?"

First, she looked as if she'd been slugged, then her brown eyes flashed fury. "I'm not even going to justify that with an answer." She grabbed the door handle. "Forget about it. I'm sorry I asked. I'm sorry about everything."

Damn, he wasn't being at all fair. She didn't deserve this much animosity. And in reality, he didn't want her to leave. "Wait."

She hesitated, the door partially ajar. "Why? So you can rake me over the coals some more because of my chosen profession?"

"No. So I can apologize."

"Apology accepted."

"Good. Now close the door."

"Why?"

"Because I need more details about what you're proposing."

She looked hopeful and sweeter than she had a right to be. "Then you'll actually consider it?"

"I'm willing to listen."

After closing the door, she settled back into the corner of the seat. "First, I'd follow you around for a week, focusing on Mitch Warner, the rancher, and his life. It's also an opportune time to reveal a lighter side of your personality. For example, what you do in your spare time. Your favorite activities. What you admire most in a woman."

"Honesty."

Again, she looked as if she'd been slapped. Why the hell couldn't he control his mouth where she was concerned? "I guess I deserve that," she said. "But I promise I'll be honest with you from now on. In fact, I'd be willing to let you see the final draft. You can approve or disapprove any of the content before it's put to bed."

Speaking of bed.... Even though he didn't like that she'd hidden the truth about her questionable occupation, Mitch was still commanded by their chemistry, and he didn't see any end to it anytime soon. Especially if she spent a solid week in his world. "What about us?"

"What about us?"

"This thing between us."

She sighed. "Our relationship would have to be strictly professional from this point forward."

"And this is supposed to sell me on the idea?"

She hinted at a smile. "Whatever's existed between us on a personal level until now will have to be ignored."

He'd bet his back forty acres she couldn't ignore it any more than he could, and he intended to put her to the test. Scooting across the seat, he cupped her chin, running his thumb over her lower lip. "You really think that's possible?"

"Sure." She didn't sound at all convinced.

He trailed his fingertip down her throat and outlined the scoop neck of her dress, following the path where his mouth had been only a few minutes before. "Just like that, you're going to turn it off?"

"Yes."

When he palmed her breast, this time through the fabric, she released a ragged breath. "Are you sure about that?" he asked.

"Positive."

"Your nipple's hard."

"It's cold."

"You're lying again."

She pulled his hand away and rested it in his lap. "I'm a lot stronger than you think. If you'll let me do this story, I'll prove it to you."

For the second time, Mitch collapsed against the seat and stared at the truck's faded headliner. "I'll have to think about."

"Fine. My plane leaves from Oklahoma City at noon. That means I'll need to leave Stella's tomorrow by 9 a.m. If you're not there, then I'll take that as a no and head back to Dallas. We'll forget any of this ever happened."

Regardless of whether he decided to do the interview, he would never forget what had happened between them last night. What had almost happened again tonight. He would never forget her. "Okay. Agreed."

She nodded toward the bar. "We need to go back inside. I'm sure they're wondering where we are."

"Suit yourself."

She frowned. "Aren't you coming in?"

"No. I'm going to say here for a while. I need to calm down."

She pinched the bridge of her nose as if she had one helluva headache. "I'm sorry I made you so angry. I never intended to do that."

"Anger isn't my problem at the moment."

She sent a pointed look at his lap, which didn't help matters at all. Even with the loose fit of the slacks, his problem was more than evident.

"Oh," she muttered then glanced away.

"Oh, yeah."

"I'm sorry about that, too."

Mitch was only sorry he couldn't do anything about it, at least not with her tonight. But maybe later. If he agreed to her request.

He had a lot to consider tonight, not only her current proposal but also the fact that he was hard as hell just thinking about what they could be doing in his bed. He'd just have to decide if having her around for a week would be worth it.

Who was he trying to fool? Damn straight it would be worth it.

When he didn't speak, she opened the truck and slid out. "I really hope I see you in the morning."

He really hoped that if he did decide to do it, he wouldn't be making a major mistake.

Tori's hope began to fade when she glanced at her watch. Half past nine, and no Mitch. She'd already mopped the kitchen floor twice in order to ready Stella's rental house for the next tenants. In fact, the family could probably eat off the vinyl tiles. And worse, she was ruining her good black slacks and favorite white crepe de chine blouse. She should have changed into something more casual but she'd wanted to save her one pair of jeans for later, in case Mitch decided to take her up on her offer. That obviously was not going to happen. Stalling for time wasn't going to make Mitch Warner magically materialize.

Last night, she'd seen him only briefly back at the bar after their tense encounter in his truck. He'd stayed long enough to toast the couple and then headed away with only a quick goodbye. He hadn't witnessed the cake-cutting, the garter toss or Tori miraculously catching the bouquet. Of course, if she hadn't made the grab, the cascading flowers would have hit her dead in the face. No doubt, the whole thing had been rigged by the bride.

And most likely, those final few moments in Mitch's presence would be her last, at least for a while. She didn't plan to return to Quail Run until after the birth of Stella's baby. She could manage that visit in a day and never even have to run into him, if she was unlucky.

Resting her palms on the top of the mop handle, Tori muttered, "Stubborn man. Stubborn, sexy man." Not only would she have to return to work without the story of the decade, she would also have to face her boss with the news that she hadn't been successful. She should've asked Mitch first before she'd called Renee yesterday morning about the possibilities. Oh, well. The plan had been a good one, even if it hadn't come to fruition.

"Time to go, Cinderella. Looks like Prince Charming isn't going to show. If we don't hurry, you'll miss your plane."

Tori looked up to see Stella standing in the hall, holding Tori's battered black duffel against her chest. She propped the mop by the back door and frowned. "You don't need to be lifting anything, Stella."

"You sound just like Bobby." She held out the bag. "Here."

Tori took the duffel and headed toward the door. She turned and scanned the house one more time, proud that she'd accomplished so much with so little sleep. The sounds of Bobby's and Stella's official consummation the night before hadn't plagued her as much as thoughts of Mitch. She doubted those would dissipate any time in the near future, even after she was back to business as usual.

Tori opened the screen and stepped out into the sunshine—then nearly fell off the porch. Leaning against his truck, Mitch Warner looked as gorgeous in the daylight as he did deep in the night. Funny, she hadn't even considered that she'd never seen him during the day. And she sure as heck hadn't considered he would actually show up considering the time. She would forgive him his tardiness. Forgive him just about anything. How could she not pardon a man in faded denim and blue flannel that matched his eyes, his arms folded over his broad chest and his long legs crossed at the ankles stretched out before him? How could she ever forget the picture he now presented? Picture. Darn, her camera was in the front seat of the car. Otherwise she might take a shot or two as a souvenir. Probably not a great idea since he wasn't exactly smiling.

When he didn't bother to move or speak, Tori strolled to Stella's car and slid her bag into the open trunk on the off chance that his sudden appearance involved a friendly visit, not a business proposition. If he had decided to nix her offer, she would be gracious. She didn't feel the need to hold anything against him—except maybe her body.

Cut it out, Tori.

If he did happen to agree to her proposal, from now on she couldn't afford to entertain any lascivious thoughts about Mitch Warner. Or at least she couldn't be obvious about it.

After Tori straightened her shoulders and closed the trunk, she turned to face Mitch. "Good morning, Mr. Warner."

He pushed off the truck and approached her slowly. "Sorry I'm late. I'm running behind this morning."

Tori's heart was running at full speed. "That's okay. Cleanup took longer than we thought." After waiting for confirmation, Tori glanced over her shoulder to find Stella had disappeared back into the house, evident by the slamming of the screen door. Some friend.

When she brought her attention back to Mitch, she noticed he'd moved closer. She also noticed that his eyes looked tired. Translucent blue, but tired. He also had a day's worth of dark beard blanketing his jaw and surrounding his lips. That would mean some heavy-duty whisker burn if she kissed him. However, she was not going to do that again, even if the temptation was stronger than the morning sun.

Tori shifted her weight and tried to relax her frame, a futile attempt at a nonchalant façade. "So what brings you here this morning?"

"You know why I'm here."

She was still too afraid to hope. "Breakfast? I have a whole-grain bar in my overnight bag."

"Are you determined to change my mind about this whole thing?"

"That depends on which way it would change. Are we going to do it?"

He grinned then, revealing dazzling white teeth accentuating his dazzling smile. "Sure. Stella's car or my truck?"

"I meant the interview."

"Too bad."

"So?"

"What do you think?"

She thought she would die on the spot from the suspense. "I don't know what to think."

He rubbed a hand over the back of his neck. "Yeah, I'll do it."

Tori kept her feet firmly fixed to keep from flinging herself into his arms. "Great. You won't regret it."

"I'm going to hold you to that."

She'd settle for him holding her. "Okay. We're agreed."

"First, I have a few ground rules I expect you to follow."

She suspected as much. "Okay."

"I don't want to answer a lot of really personal questions."

She certainly didn't intend to reveal that their first up close and personal encounter happened in the back of a truck. "Fine. I'll avoid the boxers or briefs query." She already knew the answer to that one anyway—briefs.

"And I don't want to talk about my father."

That could put a severe kink in her plans. "Mitch, we're going to have to talk about him in terms of your insistence you're not going to assume his role in politics."

"You can mention that briefly, but I don't want to talk about why we haven't spoken more than three times in fourteen years."

"Only three times?" Tori couldn't suppress the shock in her tone.

"Yeah, and that's all I'm going to say about that."

The media had speculated that father and son didn't get

along, but Tori had no idea the rift in their relationship was this acute. She made a mental note to handle that situation with fine-crystal care. "Anything else?"

He leaned forward and positioned one hand on the truck near her hip, the other in his back pocket. "Yeah. We reconsider the hands-off clause."

With him so close, Tori considered taking him up on the offer. That wasn't at all advisable. "It's necessary that we maintain a professional relationship while I'm interviewing you. Otherwise, I might lose my objectivity."

"You might gain a little more insight on my likes and dislikes, at least between the sheets."

"I don't plan to go between your sheets."

"You'd like my sheets."

"Behave yourself or *I'm* going to reconsider."

With a push of his palm, he took away his body, but not the heat that had worked its way beneath Tori's skin, as he had from the first time she'd seen him saunter into the bar like a cowboy king. "If I have to behave, I will."

She didn't believe that for a minute. "Good. Now if you'll give me an hour or so, I'll settle into the motel and then I'll have Stella give me a ride to the ranch."

"That's not going to work."

"Okay, less than an hour. I just want to change into some jeans."

His gaze raked down her, slowly, and back up again. "You look fine to me, but I meant you staying at the Quail Creek Inn. That won't work. It's a seedy place."

"Unfortunately, it's all that's available."

"You could stay in the main house." He hooked his thumbs in his pockets. "It's big enough."

Not big enough to avoid him, Tori decided. "I don't think that's a great idea."

Tori hadn't noticed Stella's reappearance until she said, "You could stay with me and Bobby."

Tori regarded her friend standing by the car's fender. "I

couldn't do that, Stella. You and Bobby are practically on your honeymoon."

Stella engaged in a little eye-rolling. "Bobby and I have been on our honeymoon for months, and if I recall, you were in the house last night."

Yes, attempting to sleep to the sounds of Stella and Bobby doing the horizontal cha-cha. "Do you have a spare room?"

"Three bedrooms but only one bath," Mitch said. "It's the original house."

"We'll manage fine," Stella said. "In fact, I'd love to have you for a little longer, Victoria. Since I've quit work, I could use the company."

Mitch sent a less-than-friendly look at Stella. "My place would be much more comfortable."

Not for Tori. Mitch Warner was the definition of temptation. Even if he slept in a galvanized steel chastity belt instead of pajamas, she could probably pick the lock with her teeth to get to him in a fit of adrenaline brought about by uncontrolled desire. She didn't trust him to keep his distance. More important, she didn't trust herself around him, especially at night.

"So what's it going to be, Tori?" he asked. "My place or Stella's?"

"Yeah, Tori," Stella said. "Which one?"

Tori felt as if she'd been thrust into an accommodation war. However, she did see certain advantages to being on Mitch's property. Rental cars were non-existent in town and she'd have to rely on Stella to cart her back and forth to the ranch every day if she stayed in the motel. That would definitely get old very quickly.

"I'll stay with Stella and Bobby."

"Then it's settled," Stella said and opened the driver's door. "Let's go. I want to be there when Bobby comes in for lunch. You can help me do a little unpacking."

Great. Tori wouldn't be a bit surprised if she was left holding a box while Bobby and Stella grabbed a nooner, just liked they'd grabbed a dawner while she'd been slaving over the floors.

When Tori rounded the car, Mitch followed her to the door. But before she could open it, he stopped her progress with a palm on the window. "If you get tired of listening to the Stella and Bobby show, come on up to my house and stay with me. I won't bother you. Much."

An hour later, she emerged from Stella's faded green sedan wearing second-skin jeans and a tight-fitting sweater—a brown-eyed angel with a she-devil body that could drive a man to his knees in worship. Mitch just might have to do that in the next few days.

Maybe Tori wasn't open to taking up where they'd left off, but that wouldn't stop Mitch from trying. Of course, she would have to be willing, otherwise it might seem that he was trading sex for a story, and he wasn't that low. But he wasn't above trying a little subtle persuasion to change her mind.

Standing on the old home place porch, Stella passed by him and said, "I'll be inside. When she gets off the phone, come on in and make yourself at home."

He turned his attention to Tori who was now conversing on a cell phone. When she laughed and tossed her hair back from one shoulder, Mitch couldn't quell the sudden jealousy. Maybe she did have a boyfriend back in Dallas. After all, she'd lied to him about her job. Okay, she hadn't exactly lied, but she had withheld the truth, at least until last night.

But if he looked at it logically, she could've led him on a merry chase, gathering information under the pretense of an extended visit, only to hightail it out of Quail Run to write a story and he wouldn't have been the wiser until it came out in print. Instead, she'd opted to be up front and honest about her plans, and he had to respect that. He wasn't quite ready to trust her, though. Not until he knew for certain she wasn't bent on making a buck on a bunch of falsehoods.

After Tori finished her conversation and opened the trunk, Mitch approached and took the suitcase from her. "Calling for backup?" he asked.

Even her frown was damn pretty in the daylight. "Calling my boss. I had to let her know I'd be staying for a week."

"She didn't have a problem with that?"

"Not when she considers what I have to gain."

Tori had no idea what she could gain if she would only say yes to him. And sure as the sun set she would say it before she left.

He set the case on the porch. "I'll leave this here for now. I want you to come up and meet my granddad."

"I've met him. I used to live here, remember?"

"Then I'm sure he'd like to see you again."

"Is that the only reason you want me in your house?"

He grinned when he noticed her blush. "What other reason would I have?"

She folded her arms beneath her breasts. "I could think of a few. I guess I'm having a little trouble trusting you."

"Guess that makes two of us."

"Good point."

He held out his hand to her, which she failed to take. He could live with that reluctance, for now. "Come on up. I'll only occupy you for a few minutes." Or longer, if she was willing.

"Okay. For a while."

At least she walked fairly close to him as they traveled up the path while he explained they owned almost three thousand acres, land that had been in his mother's family for over five generations, purchased when Oklahoma was still a territory. The conversation was so dry that by the time Mitch reached the front porch, he realized he'd missed his calling as a history professor.

"Nice house," Tori commented when he pushed open the pine door. "And very large."

"I had the Austin stone shipped from Texas, but basically it's pretty simple."

When they entered the great room, Tori looked around, her eyes wide as she honed in on the massive rock fireplace. "This is simple? The ceilings are what, twenty feet?"

"Twenty-four, and that makes the room look bigger."

She ran her hand over the brushed suede sofa. "This feels really nice."

"Kind of like the velvet last night, huh?" Mitch just couldn't help himself when he thought about her running her hand over him in the same way. He imagined taking her to that sofa and getting inside her again. He hadn't initiated that couch yet, but he just might real soon.

Or maybe not, he decided when he noticed the acid look Tori sent him over one shoulder. She turned and faced him with a strained smile. "Where's your grandfather?"

Truth be known, Mitch had no clue where Buck had gone. His '56 Chevy truck was nowhere in sight. "Guess he stepped out for a minute. I'm sure he'll be back soon. Not many places for a seventy-six-year-old widower to go in town."

Her eyes narrowed with suspicion. "Did you know he had left before you brought me up here?"

"I didn't notice his truck was gone until we got on the porch."

She sent him a skeptical look. "Are you sure?"

Man, this mutual mistrust thing wasn't going to bode well for the interview, or Mitch's plans to make love to her again. "Look, let's just get this out on the table right now. I won't question your motives, if you won't question mine."

He offered his hand again and this time she actually accepted it for a shake. "Deal."

But in that moment, neither one of them made a move to part. Mitch couldn't resist running his thumb along the smooth skin on her palm, couldn't resist hanging on a little bit longer. Obviously Tori could. She tugged away and slipped both hands into the back pockets of her jeans. He'd give a month's wages to be her hands about now.

"Anything else you want to show me?" she asked.

His grin made an appearance in spite of his effort to stop it. "You know, you might want to quit asking those kinds of questions. That would make it a lot easier for me to behave."

Her sultry smile nearly knocked the wind out of him. "My questions are innocent. I can't help it if your thoughts aren't."

"Your questions contain a lot of double entendre."

"Entendre? Now there's a word you rarely hear coming out of a cowboy's mouth."

If she only knew what other words were running around in his brain, she'd be out the door in a matter of seconds. "I know a few more. Want to hear them?"

"Would that be ranch lingo or the articulation of a Harvard grad?"

"Just simple words for a simple man." He saw more than mild curiosity in her eyes. He also saw his chance and moved a little closer. "Take sexy, for instance. That would describe you in that sweater."

A trace of self-consciousness flickered in her brown eyes. "It's blue, basic, just like me."

"How about beautiful? There's nothing basic about your beauty, Tori. It's real. Appealing. Do you want more words?"

"Why not? You're obviously on a roll."

Another kind of roll came to mind. He reached out and snagged her belt loop to pull her against him. "Tempting. That's another I don't toss around that often, but that also describes you."

"Mitch—"

He stopped her protests with a fingertip against her lips. "Dangerous. You're dangerous, Tori, in the worst kind of way, because you don't realize your power. You're deadly to a man's control."

She pulled his hand from her mouth and held it against his chest. "I could say the same thing about you and your power over women."

"That's where you're wrong. I'm not that strong, at least not around you. And you know something? I don't even begin to understand it." With his left palm, he reached down and nudged her hip until not even a scrap of air separated them. "No woman has ever done this to me so easily."

Her breath caught and her pupils flared. "Mitch, we said we wouldn't."

He ran his hand over her bottom before traveling up to the small of her back. "You said it, not me."

She wet her lips, a subtle sign of encouragement in Mitch's opinion. "What do you really want from me, Mitch Warner?"

"I want to kiss you, but only if you say yes."

He saw the hesitation in her eyes, the questions, immediately before he saw her give in and heard her whisper, "Yes."

He bent his head and brushed a kiss over one cheek, then the other, savoring the moment before he reached his ultimate goal….

"Why, looky what my grandson brung me for my birthday."

Mitch dropped his hands and hissed out an angry breath.

He'd be damned if Buck Littleton didn't have timing as bad as Bobby Lehman.

Five

Mitch's grandfather had good timing, or at least Tori assumed the pencil-thin man with the shaggy silver hair, handlebar moustache and battered straw hat was his grandfather. A long time had passed since she'd seen him and even back then, she hadn't seen him too often. He had definitely aged, but then so had they all.

Mitch stepped to her side and said, "Buck, this is Tori Barnett. She used to live in Quail Run."

Buck snatched his hat from his head and nodded. "Your mama was Cindy Barnett, Calvin Barnett's daughter, right?"

Tori managed a smile in light of her discomfort. "That's right. My granddad used to run the gas station." She wondered if Mitch had caught the fact that she had the same name as her maternal grandfather, a sure indication that her mother had never married her father.

Buck rubbed his stubbled chin. "Your mama used to do some sewing now and then for my Sally." He winked at Mitch. "Your grandma was like a race car driver on a sewing machine. She couldn't get the seams straight."

Tori was propelled back into her past by an old man's recollections. A past that had included hand-to-mouth and hard times. But her only parent had done the best that she could under the circumstances. "My mother was a very good seamstress. The best in the county."

"Last I heard, you were off to college," Buck said. "Are you back for good?"

"No. I live and work in Dallas now."

"And your mama?" he asked. "How is she faring these days?"

"She had a stroke and passed away a little over a year ago."

Buck crimped his hat in his fists. "I'm mighty sorry to hear that. She was a real good woman, as I recall."

"Yes, she was."

Mitch cleared his throat as if uncomfortable over the course of the conversation. "Tori's here to do a story on me for a magazine, Buck."

Buck's mouth opened, then snapped shut. "Well, I'll be damned. I don't know how you convinced him to do that, Tori, but it's not for me to question."

"Good." Mitch turned to Tori. "Come with me and we can get started."

Tori didn't dare ask what he wanted to start, or possibly finish. She would just follow Mitch, remind him of the rules and then silently scold herself for being proverbial putty in his presence. If she didn't grow a solid backbone soon, she'd be on her back in record time.

"Well, it was nice talking to you again, Mr. Littleton. Maybe we can have a conversation about yours and Mitch's relationship. Readers would love to know about your influence on his life."

Buck chuckled. "That's easy. I taught him how to drink beer and rope a calf and romance a woman. And if he gets out of hand, you let me know. I'll put him in his place."

Mitch took her by the elbow. "Let's go, Tori, before he starts telling more wild tales."

"Oh, and happy birthday, Buck," she tossed over one shoulder as Mitch guided her toward the adjacent hallway.

"His birthday is four months away," Mitch said as the sound of Buck's laughter followed them all the way down the corridor.

Tori counted the number of rooms, three to be exact, on the way to an unknown destination. Two were sparsely furnished, one was a bath, and all were oversized. At the end of the hall, they entered a comfortable room containing a small fireplace, battered plaid furniture, a cluttered desk complete with a computer and rows of bookshelves.

"I hang out here in the evenings," Mitch said as he closed the door behind them. "Most everything in here I've had for a lot of years."

Although she had a bad case of the nerves from being alone with him, Tori felt as if she'd discovered a treasure trove. A person could tell a lot about a man by what he kept in his private domain.

When he remained at the door, staring at her expectantly, she turned toward the shelves, grasping for something to focus on other than him. If not, she ran the risk of repeating what had almost happened before Buck's interruption. Right now, she had to concentrate on the business at hand—his interview.

"Very interesting assortment of books," she said as she perused the collection.

"I have eclectic taste."

Eclectic. Another glimpse of the Ivy League boy. Man, she corrected. Very much a man. "I can see that."

She tracked a visual path from the top shelf that held numerous Louis L'Amour books to the one below where she found several business digests. But the volume of poetry caught her immediate attention.

Tori looked back to find Mitch had taken a seat on the sofa, his tanned arm thrown casually over the back, one leg crossed over the other as if he planned to stay a while. She held up the book. "Is this a leftover from college?"

"Is there some reason why I wouldn't like a little poetry?"

Keeping her back to him, she flipped through the pages. "It

just doesn't fit your persona. I'm betting you've kept it to impress the girls."

"You're wrong."

She turned and leaned back against the shelves, the book clutched to her chest. "Prove it. Name one poem—"

"'Twice or thrice I have loved thee, before I knew thy face or name. So in a voice, so in a shapeless flame. Angels affect us oft, and worshipped be.' John Donne. From *Air and Angels.*"

Tori couldn't find her voice, couldn't find the strength to look away from his intense gaze. For the first time in a long time, she'd been stricken speechless.

He smiled, but only halfway. "Proof enough?"

"You could say that." She turned and replaced the book before facing him again. "You are certainly full of surprises, Mr. Warner. I'm very impressed."

"Haven't you heard someone recite poetry before?"

Not a to-die-for enigmatic man with a voice so strong, so resolute, so masculine that the verse had sounded like an invitation to seduction.

"My mother was a sucker for *The Itsy Bitsy Spider*. Does that count?"

He unfolded from the sofa and approached her slowly. "This was one of my mother's favorites."

Tori did well not to gasp when he brushed her arm as he reached around her. She took the weathered book he offered, *The Little Engine That Could*, opening it to the first page; yellowed from time yet holding a message that would probably never fade.

"My dear baby boy. Happy first birthday! Never let anyone tell you that you can't.—Love, Mama."

"She read that to me every night until I turned eight and decided I was too grown up to hear it again," he said, a trace of sadness in his tone. "She was a large part of my success."

A mix of emotions ran through Tori. She was flattered he had shown her something so special, and somewhat confused as to why he had. Touched by the fact that he'd kept the book all these years, and saddened by the reminder of her own mother. "My mom contributed to my success, too. She was always there when I needed her."

"I still miss mine and it's been almost fifteen years since her death."

Tori recognized that was his reason for sharing, to let her know that he could relate to her loss, her pain. A connection. Common ground. What a totally thoughtful thing to do. If not careful, she was going to take a plunge and land totally in love with this man.

"What about your father?" he asked quietly.

Tori shifted her weight from one foot to the other. "He's not in my life. Good riddance, as far as I'm concerned."

"I'm sorry."

"I'm not. My mother handled both roles very well." Tori handed him the book and sent him a shaky smile. "Life goes on, and so should this interview."

He slid the book back into place. "So when do we start the process?"

"Actually, we already have."

He frowned. "Aren't you going to take some notes?"

She tapped one finger against her temple. "Right now, I'm relying on this. Later, I will use a recorder when we get into detailed specifics and quotes."

"About the ranching business?"

"Yes, and that's next. But it's nice to know a little more about the man beneath the façade now that I've seen your choice in books."

He kept his gaze trained on her eyes. "You really think you know me by my taste in literature?"

"I know that you like westerns and probably fantasized about being a cowboy from a very early age. I know that beneath the tough guy exterior you have a poet's soul and a great love for your mother. I learned all of that in about ten minutes, tops."

"There's a lot you don't know about me, Tori." His tone sounded serious and edgy.

"I'm sure there is. And when I leave here, I still won't know everything about you. But I will know enough to do a fantastic story." She would also know the incredible high of making love with him, if only one wonderful time.

He propped one hand against the shelf above her head and leaned toward her. His expression went from solemn to seductive. "What about you, Tori? When are you going to tell me a little more about what you like?"

Considering the grainy quality of his voice, Tori decided he might as well have added "in bed" to the end of the query. His blue eyes had enough power to light an entire metropolis, enough to make Tori forget once more why she was there.

Ducking under his arm, she played nosy reporter and assessed the mess on his desk. "Let's talk about your business now."

"You're being evasive."

She turned and used the desk for support. "I'm being a journalist. Journalists interview subjects, and you are the subject, not me."

He moved in front of her, this time keeping a comfortable distance, but not far enough away to alleviate Tori's discomfort. "One of these days, I'm going to make you talk more about yourself."

"Are you going to tie me up and threaten to brand me?"

He rubbed his chin, looking thoughtful. "Hadn't thought about tying you up, but that might be interesting."

"Cut it out, Mitch, or I'll go get your grandfather to put you in your place."

"Speaking of places, I have one special place I need to show you."

"That wouldn't be down the hall, would it?"

His grin made another showboat appearance. "If you want to see *that* particular place, I'll be glad to show you any time. You just say the word."

Oh, but she wanted to say it. She wanted to find his bed and stay there with him the rest of the day and well into the night. "Thanks for the offer, but I don't think so. Now exactly where are we going?"

"Somewhere that involves both business and sex."

* * *

"We call this the Happy Place. It's where we collect semen from the bulls."

Mitch expected Tori to be somewhat shocked, as Mary Alice had been when he'd shown her the sterile room situated in the main barn. He figured the reporter might as well become accustomed to every aspect of his business, even the less than pleasant ones. But she didn't seem at all bothered by this particular setting.

Instead, she turned to him and asked, "Do you practice artificial insemination on your own herd or do you ship frozen semen? My guess is that you do both."

Mitch was more than a little bowled over by her query. "How do you know about livestock AI?"

She shrugged. "I worked part-time for a horse breeder during college. He taught me how to collect from his stallion. I can't say that it thrilled me exactly, but I learned a lot, the most important lesson being to hang on to the lead rope when you've got a stud who's hot after a teasing mare."

If Mitch had less presence of mind, his mouth would've hit the ground. "He got away?"

"Almost, but I caught him before he mounted the mare instead of the dummy. That would have been a disaster, since she was a Welsh pony and he was a seventeen-hand thoroughbred. He might have hurt her."

Even though Mitch was used to the breeding terminology, even though he'd seen both horses and bulls collected for the process of artificial insemination, it seemed kind of odd coming out of Tori's mouth, a woman with a face as innocent as they come. And considering his recent questionable state of mind, he didn't need to hear her say words like "mount" and "hot" and "teasing" either.

He swiped a hand over the back of his neck. "Guess I don't need to go into great detail about what happens then."

"No, you don't."

"Okay, then come with me back here."

He showed her to his business office, the oak paneled walls containing only his framed diploma, his desk clear of any signs of chaos, the way that he liked his life. He suspected Tori was somewhat surprised by his organization considering the demolition mess in the den.

"This is quite different from your home office," she said, confirming his suspicions.

"That's my private study I showed you earlier," he said. "Buck's in there a lot and he's not real neat. He likes to use that computer to play games and wander into a chat room now and then."

"It's nice that the Internet provides a place for senior citizens to go."

"Yeah, but he doesn't go there. He likes to hang out with the 30-something crowd. He says the old fogies are boring."

She laughed, a soft musical sound that brought back Mitch's reminiscence of the first time he'd heard her laugh. The first time he'd heard her sing. The first time—and the last time—they had made love.

Once more, his body reminded him that it only took a thought or two to propel him back into lust mode. But he was quickly realizing that with Tori Barnett, the lust was secondary to the fact that he really liked her, probably a lot more than he should. After all, she would only be here for a few more days and then they'd both go back to pursuing their careers instead of mutual pleasure. Unfortunately, she hadn't agreed to exploring that pleasure thing again—yet.

Tori slid her fingertips back and forth over the edge of the desk, causing Mitch to look away for the sake of his sanity. "You obviously have a good program going on here," she said.

That wasn't all he had going on. "Yeah. We raise a few Red Angus, the last of Buck's herd. We have two top-grade bulls and about fifty heifers for breeding."

"That's all?"

"Yeah."

"And you make a living on that?"

He bypassed her and slipped behind his desk to retrieve a business card. "Here," he said as he slid it forward.

Tori studied the card for a few minutes before raising her eyes to his. "This says L and W Consulting. What kind of consulting?"

"Cattle consulting. I've developed several methods that ensure quality stock. I employ a few men and women who go out in the field to present workshops to various ranchers all over the country. We teach them how to get the most out of their breeding programs. We also distribute instructional software and videos that I helped develop with Rand Wilson."

"Rand?"

"He's one of my ranch hands, but he's also a computer wiz."

"I assume you do this to supplement the ranch income."

"It isn't a sideline; it's a very lucrative business. I've made enough money to retire at least twice and live in Maui. I needed to put my business degree to good use. Of course, there are a few young ranchers who need a hand in getting started. I usually provide my services for free to them."

"You're an enigma," Tori said. "A true renaissance cowboy."

"I'm driven. I always have been."

And she was driving him crazy every time she looked at him, not to mention every time she nibbled on her bottom lip. What the hell was wrong with him? Could he not spend more than fifteen minutes in her presence without wanting to crawl all over her? Hell, a thirty-three-year-old man shouldn't be this wildly out of control over a woman he barely knew, even if at times he felt as if he'd known her a lot longer than three days. That was nuts.

She strolled to the small window facing the back paddock. "Well, I see a horse out there. I suppose that means you still work cattle the old-fashioned way."

Mitch walked up behind her, keeping his hands fisted so he wouldn't touch her. He needed to take this slowly from now on, otherwise she might keep running away. He didn't want her to run away. He didn't want her going anywhere in the near future except maybe into his arms again.

"That's my gelding, Ray. Buck gave him to me for my seventeenth birthday. He's on up in years, but he still has a few miles left. One of these days, I'm going to have to retire him."

"He looks like he's in great shape."

So was she, Mitch decided as he took a visual tour down her back and over her butt. She had a great body, and he had a building pressure below his belt buckle in response.

Mitch hadn't realized how close he had moved to her until Tori turned and practically ran into his chest. Deciding to give her a little space and a reason to trust him, he took a step back.

She crossed her arms over her breasts as if trying shield herself from him. "Okay, you have a successful business and a wonderful house that's probably at least four bedrooms."

"And four baths."

"You must be planning to have a large family with lots of kids."

"That has never been in my plans."

"Why?"

This was a subject he didn't really care to broach, but he needed to be honest with her now. "Because I've never put much stock in marriage."

"Your parents were happily married for quite a while, as I recall."

"Before my father…" *Whoa, Mitch.* He was getting a little carried away with his open book bit.

Her gaze didn't waver. "Before your father did what?"

Betrayed his entire family by not sticking around when he was needed most. "I don't want to talk about that."

She sighed. "I'm sorry. I didn't mean to intrude since that subject is apparently very painful for you."

Damn. She could see right through him. No one had been able to do that before, especially not a woman. But Tori was an extraordinary woman and too intuitive for Mitch's own good. "I'm over it."

"But you can't forget it, can you?"

"Tori," he said in a warning voice.

"I know. I know. Nothing too personal." She grabbed a lock of her hair and began twisting it into a spiral. "So what shall we see next?"

If Mitch had his way, he'd show her his bedroom and release all his frustration, his latent anger, in one long, hard session of lovemaking. "You need to go back to Stella's to settle in and I need to do some work."

"Can I watch for a while?"

"No. If you're in here, I won't be able to concentrate."

"I'll try to be really quiet."

And he'd be trying to silence her with his mouth. "You don't have to say anything to distract me, Tori. You only have to stand there, looking pretty."

"I'll definitely make a note of your penchant for flattery."

She had no clue about her beauty, and Mitch found that very engaging. "I don't throw out compliments that often, so accept it graciously and go visit with Stella for a while. I'll see you later."

She stuck out her lip in a pretend pout. "Okay. I guess I need to get my camera loaded anyway."

"Camera?"

"Yes, I brought it for the wedding, then promptly left it at Stella's house without taking a single picture. I have plenty of film left and that's where you'll come in."

Hell, he didn't like the sound of that. "You plan to take pictures of me?"

"Sure. A few candid shots of you and the ranch. And if you're concerned, I've taken tons of photography classes. I'm fairly good at it."

"I have no doubt about that." He had no doubt she was good at everything she endeavored.

"Normally I'd have a staff photographer come and do it, but I assumed you wouldn't want anyone else involved in this. That means you're stuck with me."

Funny, Mitch didn't feel at all stuck with her. He did feel incredibly hot at the moment, and on the verge of compromising his dignity. For a man who'd always prided himself on self-control, he was bordering on the edge of losing it big time. He collapsed into his chair and laced his hands behind his head before she caught him having a weak moment. "Get out of here, Tori, before…"

"Before what?"

Before he changed his mind, locked the door, and tried one more time to seduce her out of her sneakers, and everything else. "Before it's dinnertime and I don't get a thing accomplished today."

"Oh, but you've accomplished a lot."

"What would that be?"

"You just spent the last twenty minutes without trying to kiss me. Now that wasn't so hard, was it?"

He leaned forward and locked into her gaze. "You have no idea how hard it's been." Or how hard it was going to be as long as he wanted her this badly, and that could be for a long while.

Dinner with Stella and Bobby had been pleasant enough. The evening entertainment was not.

Tori covered her face with her hands following the first moan, then crushed the pillow over her head when the succession of name calling began.

Admittedly, tonight the love sounds bothered her on a different level. She didn't want to be reminded that if she would just say the word, she could be in Mitch's bed enjoying a little love fest of her own. In fact, she was beginning to wonder why she'd continued to fight Mitch, fight her overriding attraction to him. Sure, she should try to remain objective while gathering information. But no one would have to know what they did in the dead of night.

In reality, her resistance to intimacy with Mitch had more to do with her fear of falling for him. He wasn't really commitment material, something he had made quite clear today. Granted, he had spent nine years with one woman, but he hadn't asked that woman to marry him. No, siree, Bobby…who happened to be groaning loud enough to call the cattle home.

That did it.

Tori vaulted out of the feather bed and her feet hit the cold hardwood floor, reminding her that the weather was not conducive to taking a walk. However, she would rather face the elements than endure one more thwack of the headboard hitting the wall in a torrid tempo.

Not bothering to turn on the lamp, she snatched her robe from the bedpost and slid her feet into the ridiculous furry brown gorilla slippers Stella had given her as a gift for serving as maid of honor. The other two bridesmaids had received frogs and pigs, so she supposed she got the better end of the deal.

The floor creaked beneath her feet as she felt her way along the wall. She finally reached the small living room illuminated by a lamp in the corner—a good thing considering the area was littered with unpacked boxes. Grabbing her leather jacket from the coat tree, she yanked open the door and stepped onto the porch. The moderate breeze flowed over her and until that moment, she hadn't realized how hot she'd been. She could attribute that to the down comforter, or her own desire for Mitch that she'd warred with all day long…and most of the night.

"I figured you'd be out soon."

With her heart lodged firmly in her throat, Tori spun toward the sound of the deep voice to find a dark figure silhouetted against the limited light. She laid one shaky hand against her throat. "God, Mitch, you scared the hell out of me!"

"Sorry. I didn't mean to do that."

She walked to the glider where he now sat and hovered above him. "What are you doing here?"

"Couldn't sleep."

"And you walked all the way here to alleviate your insomnia?"

"I decided you'd probably need some company eventually."

"You were certainly taking a huge chance that I would come outside."

"Not really. I know Stella and Bobby's habits well enough

to know they'd eventually drive you out of the house. If you hadn't come out when you did, I probably would've left in an hour or two."

"An hour or two?"

His gaze raked over her in a slow excursion. "If you'd agreed to stay with me, then you wouldn't be traipsing around in the cold in your nightgown."

He was nothing if not tenacious. "Okay, I'm here, you proved your point, so you can go back to bed now."

"Not until you come back to my house with me."

"I really don't think that's necessary. They can't keep going at it all night."

"Wanna bet?"

No, she didn't, because she wasn't at all sure when Stella's and Bobby's antics might end, possibly not before dawn. "I would have my own room?"

She could see a flash of white teeth before he said, "Do you think I'm going to make you bunk with Buck?"

"That never entered my mind."

"But you thought I might offer my own room."

"That thought did cross my mind." Several times, in great detail.

"You can stay in the bedroom on the opposite side of the house from mine."

"I'm still not sure that's wise."

He released an impatient sigh. "Would you rather spend a week listening to the Stella and Bob parade on a nightly basis?"

No, she wouldn't. But she wasn't sure she could trust Mitch not to pursue the lovemaking issue. And worse, she didn't really have a lot of confidence in herself not to eventually concede.

The glider whined as he pushed out of it to stand before her. "Tori, I do solemnly swear I am not going to pull any funny stuff while you're in my house. Not if you don't want it."

She did want it, and that was the problem. Yet she didn't think she could stomach more nighttime sex noise that didn't involve her. And Mitch. "Okay. Let me just grab a few things and I'll spend the night tonight."

He inclined his head. "Only tonight?"

"That depends."

"On what?"

"On whether you behave yourself."

"The door has a lock. Then you can be assured I won't bother you while you're sleeping."

Predictably, he hadn't said he would adhere to that when she wasn't sleeping. "Fine. I'll be right back."

As she pulled open the screen, Mitch said from behind her, "Nice slippers."

She turned and stuck out a gorilla-covered foot. "Yeah, I like to monkey around now and then."

He gave her a crooked smile. "Oh, yeah?"

Releasing a groan, she turned away from all that charisma and hoped she had enough strength to keep turning away for the remainder of the week.

Mitch felt a little guilty over being grateful that Bobby had a penchant for hamming it up in the bedroom. But Tori really would be more comfortable in his house. She'd also be nearby in case she changed her mind.

"This is it," he told her as he pushed open the door. "Nothing fancy, but it does have its own bathroom."

Tori walked into the room still wearing her leather jacket over her nightclothes. When the light hit the pale blue gown, he could see the outline of her bare legs all the way to her thighs beneath the sheer fabric. Best not to look there if he intended to go back to his own room and get some sleep.

She set her duffel down on the red plaid spread and faced him. "It looks comfortable enough."

"The bed was from my room in the old house but it has a new mattress." Mitch was having a hard time not looking at her breasts.

When Tori clutched the jacket closed, he realized he'd been

caught. "You know, the old house is nice enough," she said. "Why did you build a new one?"

The memories had been too much for Mitch to bear—memories of the time he'd spent with his mother during the summers when his dad had been too busy for them both. Memories of the last days of her life. Too many ghosts, and facts that Tori didn't need to know, even though he had the strongest urge to tell her.

Instead, he said, "I wanted something that was solely my contribution to the ranch, a symbol of my putting down roots here. Buck was resistant at first, but I finally talked him into living here and letting Bob use the old place instead of staying with the other hands in the bunkhouse out back. He did insist we bring in some of the furniture so he'd feel more at home."

Tori pointed at a picture hanging on the opposite wall. "Did he insist on that, too?"

Mitch moved closer to her to see what had caught her attention. Damn. He'd forgotten all about that stupid photo of him on a pony wearing a red felt cowboy hat, complete with a jockey string cinched beneath his chin and matching red chaps. "Yeah, that was definitely his idea."

"Nice outfit," she said, grinning. "I think it's adorable."

He could say the same about her with those damned ape house shoes hugging her feet. He gestured toward the closet. "You can hang your stuff in there."

She glanced at the bag on the bed. "I didn't bring that much stuff. Since I wasn't planning on staying, I'll have to borrow some clothes from Stella."

Right now, he'd like to help her shed her clothes. "Tomorrow, you can bring whatever else you need."

She propped both hands on her hips. "Now what makes you so sure I'm going to stay here for the remainder of my visit?"

"Because you want to get some sleep."

"True, I do." She stretched her arms and yawned, causing the jacket to gape, revealing the outline of her breasts and the shading of her nipples.

If he didn't get out soon, there was no telling what he might do. "If there's nothing else you need, I'll go to my room now. Buck's two doors down, but he shouldn't bother you."

"Actually, I do need something from you." She perched on the end of the bed and patted the mattress. "Come here."

Before he could sit, she pointed a finger at him. "I only want to talk, so get rid of that look on your face."

He scowled. "What look?"

"The one you always give me when you have certain things on your mind."

Good going, Mitch. He might as well have I Want You, Tori tattooed on his forehead. "Fine. I won't look at you." He didn't dare sit by her, either, not if he wanted to control himself. "I'll just stand here and you talk."

"All right. I have an idea I want to run past you."

If it didn't involve them assuming a prone position, he wasn't sure he wanted to hear it. "Okay. Shoot."

"I've been thinking about us, our relationship, and I've decided we need to start over."

"Start over?"

"Yes. As friends. Maybe then we won't be so inclined to skip ahead to the next step."

"We've already gone way beyond the next step, Tori. We can't go back." Nor did he want to. He wouldn't take back one moment of their first night together.

"It's all a mindset, Mitch. Besides, we do have a few things in common, a good basis for a friendship."

Mitch could think of one in particular—they were damn good together in bed. Or at least in the bed of a truck, since they hadn't actually made it into a real bed. "What things?"

"We've both lost our mothers."

"True." Their shared loss had made him feel even closer to her. "What else?"

"We like to dance."

"Friends don't dance, at least not as close as we do. You're going to have to do better than that."

She sat silent for a moment, then snapped her fingers and pointed. "I've got it. We both know about the breeding process."

Mitch couldn't help smiling over Tori's obvious chagrin. "Yeah, we do."

"You know what I mean. Anyway, I think if we build on that friendship, then when I leave here, we'll both be the better for it."

In other words, she was saying she wanted nothing more than friendship. That should have been okay with Mitch, but for some reason, it wasn't. "I've never really had a woman friend before."

"You and Mary Alice weren't friends?"

He could've gone all night without Tori mentioning her. "Maybe years ago, when we were younger. But basically, we didn't talk all that much."

"I see."

Mitch was surprised by her sober tone. "Mary Alice and I are over. We should've been over a long time ago."

She leaned back on her bent elbows, thrusting her breasts forward and adding to Mitch's increasing discomfort. "Why did you finally break it off after nine years?"

He wasn't sure he needed to go there, either, but it would be better if Tori knew up front his opinion on the subject wasn't bound to change. "She wanted to get married and as I've told you, marriage isn't something I plan to undertake."

"Did you love her?" Mitch could tell she regretted asking when she looked away and said, "Never mind. That's none of my business."

No, it wasn't, but he wanted her to know the reality of his relationship with Mary Alice. Taking a huge risk, he sat on the edge of the mattress, keeping his hands clasped together between his parted knees. "She didn't want me exactly. She wanted my money and my name. She's always been that way. When I didn't bend to her will, she went looking for someone who would, namely Brady Stevens."

"Now he's quite a catch."

"Yeah. He always kind of reminded me of an anemic perch."

Tori's laughter started out as a chuckle then grew into a full-fledged guffaw. Mitch tried to refrain from joining her, but he couldn't.

"Cut it out in there!" came the very irritable voice of Buck.

Tori slapped her hand over her mouth until she recovered. "I'm so sorry. I forgot about your grandfather."

"Don't worry about him. In fact, I'm not sure he's really awake. He's been known to talk in his sleep."

"Does he walk in his sleep?"

"No. And if you're worried, neither do I."

"I'm not worried." She glanced at the bedside clock. "Speaking of sleep, it's past one. We both need to go to bed."

"I'm all for that."

"Alone."

Double damn.

Mitch rose from the bed then faced her. "I'll think about the friends thing." When he wasn't thinking about making love to her.

"It's not going to be that difficult, I promise. In fact, I'll prove it."

Taking Mitch by surprise, she came off the bed and wrapped her arms around him. "See? We're hugging and that's all it has to be."

He kept his frame as stiff as a split-rail fence post and his arms loosely around her. Right now it would take him a split second to back her up and lay her down on the bed so he could try a little urging.

She stood on tiptoe and kissed his cheek. "Good night, Mitch. Sweet dreams."

The sweetest dream was in his arms, but he wouldn't make a move now. If she wanted to be friendly, he could do that. At least tonight. He swept her bangs away and kissed her forehead. "'Night, Tori."

Again, neither of them moved away, same as it had been earlier that day. And the real shocker came when Tori, who'd insisted on friendship only a few moments earlier, grabbed his neck and brought his lips to hers.

As far as kisses went, this one had little to do with simple friendship. Simple need, yes. It was hot. It was deep. It was killing Mitch not to take it further.

Tori pushed away first and Mitch held up his palms. "That was not my fault."

She slid both hands through her hair. "I know. It was mine. It won't happen again."

Mitch headed for the door but before he walked out, he turned to her and said, "You just keep telling yourself that, Tori. Maybe then you'll start to believe it."

Six

She could not believe she'd been such a fool.

That was the first thought that entered Tori's mind when the un streaming into the window hit her face. She'd been a com-lete and absolute idiot last night. What had possessed her to iss Mitch after she'd been so adamant about establishing a riendship with him? Well, that was obvious. Mitch had pos-essed her since the night she'd met him. The little devil.

Rolling to her side, she checked the clock, then bolted up-ight. Almost noon. Why hadn't Mitch woken her? Probably ecause he was determined to avoid her after her behavior last ight. She sure as heck couldn't blame him. But on the other and, she wasn't going to let him. She still had a job to do.

After a quick shower, she completed her morning routine nd then slipped on a plain gray sweatshirt and a pair of Stel-a's low-riding, pre-pregnancy jeans. They were a little loose, ut they would have to do since Tori hadn't brought enough asual clothes to last through the week.

After slipping on a pair of sneakers, she hurried into the living room to find it deserted. The kitchen showed no signs o life with the exception of a couple of coffee cups and a dis carded copy of the weekly *Quail Run Herald* on the dinett table. Although she was sorely tempted to peruse the news an find out if anything had been added to the usual gossip, sh didn't have time. Her next stop would be the barn in hopes tha she could catch a few minutes with Mitch.

Tori left the house and walked the path at a fast clip, admit tedly driven by anticipation and excitement over seeing hin again. When she caught sight of several men gathered in th arena adjacent to the barn, she pulled up short. She walked t the pen and propped one foot on the bottom rung, shading he eyes against the sun to survey the activity. Two cowboys o horses turned profile conversed with the other onlookers stand ing near the roping chute. One of those cowboys happened t be Mitch Warner.

His long leg, the one she could see, dangled at the horse' side, bypassing the stirrup. He had one large hand draped ca sually on the saddle horn, the other resting on his thigh encase in faded jeans. He wore a black felt hat, a pair of brown rough out boots and a confidence that couldn't be ignored, even at thi distance. Tori cursed the fact she still hadn't retrieved her cam era because this picture was definitely worth a thousand words

Old West magnificence. Raw machismo. Undeniable mag netism.

Mitch Warner was all those things and more.

Tori tried to overlook the sudden rush of heat, the heady bou of chills, the desire for him that never seemed to let go. In he head, she knew it would be best to return to Stella's and wai until later to catch up with him. In her heart, she knew sh couldn't leave. Not yet. Not until she had a longer look, befor someone noticed her presence.

Too late, she realized when Buck sauntered around the pe and headed toward her with a bowlegged gait.

"Hey, missy," he said as he stood next to her, one ragtag boo propped on the rung not far from her foot.

"Hey, Buck." She nodded toward the gang who so far had failed to heed her appearance. "Are they about to brand a calf?"

"Nope. They've been playin' all morning. Breakaway roping just for the fun of it."

"I'm not sure I understand the 'breakaway' part."

"They rope the calf, then let go of the rope. Then a man goes into the pen, takes the rope off the calf and they do it all over again. Best time wins."

"What do they win?"

"Braggin' rights. That's about it. Most of those boys don't have all that much. Mitch employs as many as he can full-time. Sometimes he gives the others part-time work when he has something extra he needs done. Next week, they'll help him move the rest of the herd in closer to the barns before winter sets in. Easier to feed them that way."

Tori surveyed the motley crew, men of all shapes, sizes and ages. Then she noticed the twenty-something man on the horse next to Mitch, a ruggedly handsome man with massive shoulders, longish golden hair and a winning smile. But her attention was soon drawn to what he was missing—his right arm below his elbow. "Does he work here?" she asked Buck, pointing to the cowboy.

Buck chuckled. "Yeah. We call him Bandit, for one-armed bandit."

Tori frowned. "That seems kind of cruel."

"Nah. He's the one that started it. It kind of describes his way with the ladies. He's been known to steal their.... Well, never mind about that."

Tori laughed. "He sounds like an interesting guy."

"He's a good guy. Back when Gus came to visit during the summer, he'd follow Gus around like a pup looking for a teat. After Rand—that's his real name—lost his arm when he was sixteen, Gus kind of adopted him, taught him how to rope with one hand and his teeth. It's the strangest sight you'll ever see."

Rand, the software developer Mitch had mentioned yesterday. "He's the computer expert?"

"Yeah, but he wanted to be a horse vet. Even went to school and came close to finishing before he quit. He said it wasn't for him, but we figure it was too much for him to handle, with his missing arm and all."

Tori suspected there was quite a story there, but she had to concentrate on the one that presently needed her attention. "Why do you call Mitch 'Gus'?"

"At first I called him 'Grumpy Gus' cause he was so grumpy as a boy. Damn serious from the day he was born. 'Course, I could make him laugh by showing him my teeth." Buck thrust a partial containing his top two teeth out with his tongue, then shoved them back in the same way.

"Ouch," was all Tori could think to say.

"Don't hurt a'tall. Now when that horse kicked me in the mouth, it hurt somethin' fierce."

She wrinkled her nose. "I can imagine."

She could also imagine why Mitch was so fond of this man. Buck was salt of the earth, as good as gold, and those kind of men were hard to come by in this day and time. Obviously his grandson had picked up some of those same traits, considering he was inclined to hire the down-and-out from town. That must have been what Mary Alice had meant when she'd said Mitch was kind to the common folk. To look at him now, he appeared just as common. To know him as she was beginning to know him, he was anything but common—in appearance, in personality, in his ability to mesmerize, as he was doing right then when he rode around the pen, looping the rope with both hands and guiding the horse with the sheer strength of his legs.

She was vaguely aware that Buck had said something, but in her daze, she hadn't heard a thing. Tearing her gaze away from Mitch, she said, "Huh?"

"I said he's a good man."

"I'm sure he is." She knew he was.

"All he needs is a good woman."

Tori continued to watch Mitch in an effort not to appear too interested as he chased after a calf someone released from the chute. "I'm sure he'll find one eventually."

"I'm beginning to wonder. He wasted nine years on the wrong woman."

Only then did she turn to Buck. "You weren't disappointed when it didn't work out between him and Mary Alice?"

"Nah. She's too prissy. Gus needs someone who understands him. Not too many gals around here to choose from."

She gave her attention back to Mitch. "I'm sure that's true. It's a small town."

Tori sensed Buck staring at her in the moments of passing silence before he said, "How long do you plan to stay?"

"Until Sunday."

"I couldn't talk you into staying longer?"

She glanced at him briefly. "I have a job and an apartment waiting for me back in Dallas."

"You got a boyfriend?"

She dropped her foot from the rung and leaned one shoulder against the rail to face him. "Now, Buck, you know you're much too young for me."

In his grin, she saw a glimpse of his grandson. "Yeah, but you ain't too old for Gus. He could use a woman like you, someone to keep him grounded."

"You don't even know me."

"I know you well enough, Tori. You're like him. You're smart and you hung in there when people weren't so nice to you."

"Why do you think people weren't nice to me?"

"I know about your mama and how she never got married. I heard a few people talk, but I was never one to pass judgment on anyone. You don't know a person's situation till you've walked in their shoes."

She lowered her eyes and studied the dried grass beneath her feet. "It wasn't bad all the time. I have a few very good memories. But I've since moved on. I don't intend to live here permanently again."

"This town ain't so terrible, as long as you have someone to lean on when the going gets tough."

The crowd scattered and headed away in all directions, while Mitch dismounted and started toward the barn. Tori saw that as an excuse to avoid any further matchmaking attempts by Buck, as well as her chance to finally talk to Mitch. She patted Buck's shoulder and smiled. "Got to get some work done now. I guess I'll see you later."

"You can go with me to the fair if that grandson of mine won't take you."

"Fair?"

"The Harvest Festival. You remember that. Happens the same time every October and ends with the rodeo this weekend."

Once more, Tori was thrust back into her past. She'd been conceived following that rodeo almost twenty-eight years ago, the only thing she knew about how she had come to be, and her father—a roving rodeo bum. "I remember, but I hadn't thought about going."

"You need to go. Best barbecue and beer in the state. Not that I touch the stuff."

Tori grinned. "You expect me to believe that?"

"Nope, but you do need to believe one thing." He pointed at the barn and closed one eye as if preparing to take a shot. "That boy in there has it bad for you."

Tori couldn't think of any response, so she gave him only a friendly goodbye as she walked away to seek out Mitch.

Mitch had it bad for *her*? Not hardly. Maybe her body, but that was it. On the other hand, she was starting to have it bad for him, and that might not be so good.

But it could be so good, if she continued to weaken in his presence. And if the devastating cowboy kept pressing the issue, she had no doubt her resolve would eventually wane.

After rinsing Ray off, Mitch stepped out of the wash rack to find Tori leaning back against the opposing stall. She had her hair pulled into a ponytail high atop her head and the sweatshirt she wore looked like a jogger's reject. The jeans were too big, and if she wasn't the cutest thing he'd ever seen, he'd eat his roping saddle for lunch.

She lifted her hand in a flat-palm wave. "Hi. Got a few minutes to spare?"

He'd give her a few minutes. Hell, he'd give her hours if she would just give it up and acknowledge they wanted each other. He could see it in her dark eyes, feel it in his bones. The heat between them was so fierce that it could fry the shavings in the stalls.

"Sure. I'll just leave Ray tied up until he dries. We can go into my office."

Tori followed behind him, keeping her distance even after they were tucked away behind a closed door. She hadn't noticed that he'd locked it, but if she had, he would offer the explanation that anyone was bound to come in, and he didn't want to interrupt the interview. That sounded logical, even if it was a stretch in the truth department.

He'd stayed up most of the night, literally up, hard and aching for her. That ache had yet to subside, nor would it until he made love to her again, this time with slow precision, until he'd convinced her that answering their mutual need was only natural.

While Tori stood with her arms folded tightly over her middle, Mitch claimed a seat on the edge of his desk.

"Did you sleep well?" he asked, thinking that was the most innocuous thing he could say at the moment.

"Obviously. You should've gotten me up earlier."

He'd wanted to rouse in ways that she could only imagine but had resisted with the little scrap of will he had left. "I figured you needed your rest. Besides, this is the only time I've had a break since dawn."

She nodded at the computer. "What are you doing there?"

"Tracking the herd and adding in a couple of new calves into the program. They all have numbers."

"They should have names."

"If you can come up with twenty-three, then have at it."

"That could be a challenge, I guess."

The challenge right now came when she wet her lips. Mitch had to grip the edge of the desk to keep from grabbing her and kissing her into mindlessness. "Anything else you want to know about the business?"

Her gaze shifted to the diploma hanging on the wall to her right. "I'm sure I'll think of something, but first, I want to apologize for my behavior last night."

He was tired of both hearing and voicing those words. Tired of fighting their attraction. "When's it going to stop, Tori?"

She centered her gaze on him. "It won't happen again."

"I meant our apologies for wanting each other. Maybe it's time we just quit saying we're sorry and accept the fact that this thing is stronger than both of us."

"It's not, Mitch. We're adult enough to control ourselves."

"This has nothing to do with how old we are. It has everything to do with how hot we are for each other."

"You certainly are making some fairly big assumptions."

"Assumptions or truths?"

"Assumptions."

Mitch pushed away from the desk and moved closer to her. "You're not even a little bit hot and bothered right now, knowing we're alone? Knowing we could do anything we please and not a soul would know about it?"

"No." She turned away from him and walked to the window, but not before he saw the uncertainty in her expression, the desire in her eyes.

He came up behind her and this time, he didn't bother to keep his hands off of her. He couldn't.

Circling his arms around her waist, he pulled her against him. She didn't resist, but she also didn't relax. "I don't believe you, Tori. I think right now, you're about to go up in flames. So am I."

"I'm about to go up to Stella's and get my camera."

He worked her sweatshirt up and rested his palm on her bare abdomen. "I wouldn't mind taking a few pictures as long as we do it without our clothes."

Her breath hissed out when he began to trace the waistband on the loose-fitting jeans with a fingertip. "Not a good idea. They could fall into the wrong hands."

Mitch slid his palm right beneath the jeans until he contacted the band on her panties. "I'd make sure they stayed in my hands."

"Mitch, we can't." Tori tipped her head back against his shoulder, belying her protest.

He inched his palm lower, beneath the lace. "You don't have to do anything, Tori, except enjoy it."

The gasp that slipped out of her mouth was soft, needy, and so was her flesh as he searched for the place that would ensure her pleasure.

"You're hot, Tori," he told her as he caressed her with his fingertips, his strokes deliberate in their intent. He wanted her weak and wanting. He wanted to hear her moan, feel her come apart.

When the rap sounded at the door, Tori yanked his hand from beneath her jeans and wrenched away.

"Hey, Mitch, are you in there?"

Mitch walked to the desk, braced both palms on the edge and lowered his head. "Yeah, Bob. I'm here." He sounded winded, something that wouldn't be lost on his foreman.

"Is Tori with you?"

"Yes," she answered in a raspy voice. "We were just talking."

Bobby chuckled. "Okay. Stella wanted me to tell you she's made some lunch, so when you and Mitch are done *talking*, come on up."

"She'll be there in a minute, Bob," Mitch answered for her.

"If it's only going to take you a minute, Mitch, then maybe you should grab something to eat so you'll have more stamina."

One more word and Mitch was going to rearrange his foreman's face. "Get out of here, Bob."

"I'm leaving, boss. Take your time, Tori." Bobby's retreating footsteps could barely be heard over his laughter.

"Mitch, I'm—"

"Don't say it, Tori. Don't you dare say you're sorry."

"I was going to say I'm totally losing my mind."

He shoved back from the desk and faced her. "Join the club."

She linked her hands behind her neck, causing the sweatshirt to ride up where Mitch caught a glimpse of her navel. He did not need to see anything that even resembled bare flesh.

Dropping her arms to her side, she blew out a slow breath. "Okay. Maybe this thing is stronger than both of us."

"What clued you in? Was it before or after I almost made you—"

"Before."

"What are we going to do about it?" he asked even though he knew exactly what he wanted to do—carry her up to the house and into his bed.

"Well, right now, I'm going to get some lunch, then I'm going to write down a few notes."

He allowed a disparaging smile to surface. "Until we finish what we started a minute ago, your notes are going to be incomplete."

She came as close to a scowl as Mitch had witnessed so far. "Notes as in your business skills."

He took two steps toward her. "That's not going to be as interesting."

She smiled and took two steps back. "I've got a great idea. Mitch Warner's ten favorite ways to please a woman."

He advanced one more step. "Only ten?"

This time, she didn't move. "You know, I don't think you really want to go there in the article. You'd never have a moment's peace for all the women lining up the drive to find out if you live up to the hype."

One more step and he'd be in her face, and back into trouble. "Do I live up to the hype?"

She hesitated and pretended to think a moment. "I'm not sure yet. As you've said, my notes are still incomplete."

Five more minutes of this kind of talk and he was going to

back her up against the wall, to hell with the bed. "Maybe we should do some more research tonight."

"Your granddad invited me to the festival."

Mitch had totally forgotten about the event that he'd attended for the past ten years without fail. "I'll go with you."

"You will?"

"Yeah. You probably need some protection from all the cowboys. Once they get a good look at you, you'll be fighting them off in record numbers."

"Yeah. Sure."

"I'm serious, Tori. It's not too often that a woman as good-looking as you comes into town." And he'd be damned if he'd let any of them touch her.

"And who is going to protect me from you?"

Man, he'd really done it now if she was that wary of him. "You don't have to worry about that. I'll be on my best behavior."

She walked up to him, adjusted his collar and then patted him on his chest. "We could consider this a friendly date."

"A date?"

"Does Mitch Warner not date?"

The last real date he'd been on had been a wreck—dinner with Mary Alice and her daddy. Clyde Marshall had spent the entire evening blowing cigar smoke in Mitch's face while he'd tried to sell Mitch on the benefits of becoming a member of the family. "I might shock a few people in town if I stroll in with you on my arm."

Her expression sobered. "No one has to know it's actually a date, Mitch, if that's what's worrying you."

"I didn't say I cared what anyone thought."

"You might, considering you'll be with me."

He didn't understand this one damn bit. "You're not making any sense, Tori."

She sighed. "When I was younger, people assumed that since my mother had me out of wedlock, I would automatically follow in her footsteps. I heard the speculation many times before I got out of this godforsaken town. For that reason, I didn't date. I didn't give anyone any reason to believe that I was anything but a good girl who didn't dare step out of line."

Now it was beginning to make sense. On one level, she was the self-assured career woman. On a deeper plane, she was still that vulnerable teenager trying to prove her worthiness to walk among society. "Then you're saying I might not want to be seen with you because people might assume that you, a grown woman, might be sleeping with me?"

"Something like that."

"Tori, you don't have anything to prove to me or anyone else. Whatever happens between us is our business, and no one else's. It doesn't make you a bad person." When she lowered her head, he lifted her chin. "I would be honored to escort you through the streets of town. To hell with what anyone thinks."

Her smile illuminated the room, and something in Mitch lit up, too. It felt good to bring out that smile with such a simple gesture. Unlike Mary Alice, it took so little to please Tori, only one more reason why he enjoyed her company. One more reason to show her more pleasure than she'd ever known.

"Great," she said. "I'll get to work, you get to work then we'll go to the fair. What time?"

"Seven. I'll pick you up."

Her smile withered. "Are you sure you want to do this? I could always go with Stella and Bobby or Buck."

He brushed a kiss across her cheek. "I wouldn't do it if I didn't want to. I don't do anything I don't want to do." Except he didn't want to feel what he was feeling for Tori, but it seemed he had little choice in the matter.

"Okay. I'll see you at seven," she said, followed by a quick kiss on his cheek.

When she turned and headed for the door, he said, "One more thing, Tori."

She faced him with her hand curled around the knob. "What?"

"You and I both know that what's going on between us isn't going to change anytime soon."

"And your point?"

"Would it be so wrong to just enjoy each other while you're here?"

"Why don't we wait and see how it goes tonight?"

He knew exactly how it was going to go. He'd be pretending that everything between them was casual, but deep down he would be wanting her with every breath he drew. "All right. I can live with that." If it didn't kill him.

"Fine. I'll see you later."

When Tori closed the door, Mitch dropped down into the chair behind his desk and rested his face in his hands. He couldn't help but wonder if his behavior, his uncontrolled desire for her, had her believing that he saw her as an easy target because of her history. Very far from the truth.

Tori Barnett was smart and sexy. A class act. A woman that any man with half a brain would like to know better. He had revealed more about himself to her than he'd ever revealed to any woman. She'd begun to melt his emotional walls and although he found that troublesome, he couldn't ignore the anticipation every time she walked into a room—and that had little to do with sex, as reluctant as he was to admit it.

Yet he had offered her no more than a date to the local shindig and a few sessions of lovemaking while she was in town. But then she hadn't asked anything else of him. Still, he intended to put on the brakes. Tonight, he would treat her like the one-in-a-million woman she was. He wouldn't expect more than her company and, in turn, prove that he did respect her enough to ignore his own needs. Anything that happened between them from this point forward would be up to her.

He would be the gentleman his mother had taught him to be. In the meantime, he would remind himself that in a matter of days, she would leave him to return to her own life. He would also try to ignore that bite of regret struggling to the surface every time he thought about her departure.

He still had six days in her presence and even if they never made love again, Mitch would always be glad for this time with Tori Barnett—an honest-to-goodness good girl.

"Bobby tells me you were doing Mitch in his office."

Tori stopped mid-bite and swallowed quickly in order to deliver a retort to her former best friend. "I was not *doing* Mitch anywhere."

Stella pushed her plate back and smiled. "And why weren't you, Tori?"

"Oh, good grief." Snatching her own plate from the table, Tori walked to the kitchen counter, shoved the uneaten half of her turkey sandwich into the trash, then set the dish in the sink. "Give me one good reason why I should be sleeping with Mitch Warner."

"Because you want to."

Exactly, Tori thought, staring into the suds as if they could foretell the future. "What I might want to do and what I should do are two different things."

"Tori, don't you think it's time to stop being the good girl?"

How weird that Stella should bring that up considering Tori's recent conversation with Mitch. For a second, she wondered if they'd been plotting the demise of her resistance together. "If you recall, I was not a *good girl* four nights ago."

Stella came up beside Tori and rested an elbow on her shoulder. "Knowing you, you've been beating yourself up inside ever since."

Tori shrugged off Stella's arm and began washing the dishes with a vengeance. "I haven't exactly been beating myself up, although I probably should."

"Why? What happened between you and Mitch was nature having a field day. You should be glad you've had the opportunity, and you should be trying to grab a few more."

She ran the dishrag round and round in a glass until it squeaked. "To what end, Stella? I'll be leaving here in a few days and then it's over."

"So?"

A stretch of silence passed before Stella said, "Oh, gosh. You're falling in love with him!"

"I'm not. I can't."

"Sometimes you don't have a choice. I certainly didn't want to fall in love with Bobby, but I'm glad I did." She patted her belly. "Now I have a baby on the way and a man who loves me more than his horse."

Tori chuckled. "That's nice to know, but that's exactly the reason why I can't fall for Mitch. He doesn't love me more than his horse, and he never will."

"He could. Stranger things have happened."

After rinsing off one plate, Tori leaned a hip against the counter and faced Stella. "Not with Mitch. He gives the term 'confirmed bachelor' a whole new meaning. His determination to avoid commitment is etched in cement."

"Then my advice is to make a few memories to take back to Dallas with you. If you're going to fall in love with him, you'll do that without going to bed with him again. You can't make it any worse by having a little fun while you're falling."

Stella was probably right. If she was going to lose her heart to Mitch, she would do that without ever kissing him again.

Until this point in her life, she'd been a model citizen. She didn't even have a citation on her driving record. She'd been a devoted daughter. She'd waited until she'd been in a long-term relationship before she'd made love for the first time. She'd walked the straight and narrow for so long she was surprised she didn't step heel to toe. Enough was enough.

Saint Victoria vowed to say goodbye to the good girl, at least for tonight.

Seven

The fair had packed the streets to capacity, both with vendors and townsfolk from across three counties. As it had been from the time Tori was young, all the citizens looked forward to the event as a nice diversion from the everyday grind. Back in her youth, she'd always attended the festivities with her friends. Not once had she ever been on the arm of a boy, taking in the games on the midway provided by the same Oklahoma City carnival company for fifty years. Not once had she sat in Horner's pasture on a blanket with a date to watch the fireworks light up the sky after sundown. Not once had she kissed on a Ferris wheel.

Those were nothing more than unrealized teenage dreams. Tonight she enjoyed the company of a dream man dressed in a starched pale blue shirt that enhanced his eyes, just-right jeans that highlighted his attributes and a tan felt hat that crowned him the consummate cowboy. And his cologne—well, that should just be labeled lethal.

Yes, tonight Tori walked the sidewalk amidst the chaos of

the crowd, the gorgeous Mitch Warner by her side—when he wasn't shaking hands with all the passersby. His political roots were showing, whether he cared to admit it or not. She wouldn't be a bit surprised if he started kissing babies. That was okay, as long as he saved a few for her later on.

Right then she stood on the sidewalk in front of the hardware store, waiting while Mitch visited with Lanham Farley, the town's mayor who happened to be older than Red River dirt. However, he was still upright and able to take nourishment, evident by the fact he was gnawing on a smoked turkey leg with his dentures.

Tori engaged in people watching to pass the time. She had to admit the excitement in the air was palpable. Strident screams came from the vicinity of the belly-flopping rides scattered around on the vacant lot at the end of the street. That lot used to house the livestock auction barns before people took their business to bigger cities and better markets. She was amazed that Quail Run hadn't completely died out as so many small towns had. In many ways, she was glad it hadn't, even if she never planned to live here again. As she'd told Buck earlier that day, not every memory was a bad one. And she hoped tonight that with Mitch, she might make a few more good ones. If he ever escaped the esteemed mayor.

"Well, my, my, you did stick around."

Tori glanced to her right to see Mary Alice Marshall, her jeans painted on her narrow hips and her lips painted fire-engine red. Her perfectly curled long blond hair trailed from beneath a white cowboy hat as she clutched an armful of stuffed animals that Tori would like to tell her to stuff in a place where the sun don't shine. "Hello, Mary Alice. Looks like you made a haul."

Mary Alice squeezed the animals to her ample chest. "Actually, Brady won these for me. Aren't they cute? I plan to give them to the children's home in Bennett."

"That's nice."

"And it's nice of you to support the festival, considering your limited means. But you shouldn't just stand here." She pulled a strip of red tickets from the pocket of her jeans. "Take these and go have some fun."

Tori intended to, starting now. "Actually, I'm waiting for Mitch, so I won't be needing any freebies."

"Mitch?" Mary Alice's voice cracked like an adolescent boy's.

"Yes." She nodded toward the cowboy-in-question. "He's talking to Mayor Farley. I'm sure he'll be finished in a moment."

Mary Alice inclined her head and gave Tori a hard stare. "Are you and Mitch an item, or is he just being charitable?"

Tori gritted her teeth to halt the litany of insults threatening to spew forth. "Actually, he's—"

"Ready to go."

Mitch's surprise appearance couldn't have been better timed. The arm he draped over Tori's shoulder couldn't have been more welcome. "Let's go, Tori." He touched the brim of his hat and said, "'Night, Mary Alice," but didn't wait for a response.

Tori sent Mary Alice a smug smile over one shoulder as they walked away. "Have a good time with Brady."

After they'd traveled a block, Mitch asked, "What did she say to you?" concern in his voice and his eyes.

"Nothing much. She just wanted to make sure I remembered my place and wished me a good time, until she found out I'm having it with you."

"She's just blowing steam."

"She still has a thing for you."

"She's jealous of you, but it's not only because you're with me."

A perfect blonde with big breasts and more money than God was jealous of her? "That's a stretch, Mitch."

"That's the truth. Believe me, I've known her a long time, and I can see envy written all over her face. She covets your independence because she wanted to leave here, just like you, but she was too afraid of her father to make a move."

"That's really a shame."

"That's the past and I want to forget about it and her."

When Mitch dropped his arm from around her, Tori couldn't ignore the disappointment. But then he took her hand and said, "Let's go play some games on the midway. I usually win."

And Mitch did at the basketball toss on the first try.

The carnie pointed to the myriad stuffed animals clipped to a string above their heads. "Which one do you want, little lady?"

Tori studied them for a few moments but before she could make her choice, Mitch said, "She'll take the monkey."

"One monkey it is," the carnie said as he handed Tori the miniature ape with a yellow plastic banana glued to his hand.

Tori gave Mitch a bewildered look as he took her by the arm and guided her past the fortune teller booth. "I was about to pick the white tiger."

"I thought the monkey complemented your house shoes."

Holding the ape up, she said, "You're right. And he needs a name."

"He reminds me of the mayor, so you should call him Lanham."

Tori laughed. "You're right. Lanham it is. Lanny for short."

Once more, Mitch draped an arm around her shoulder. "What now?"

"I want some cotton candy."

"I can do that."

She waited near the stand while Mitch waited in line. Several people passed by her and stared, but she couldn't say that she recognized any of them. And she doubted anyone recognized her, considering how long it had been since she'd been in town. Still, she suspected that their covert glances had to do with her "date" tonight. Before she returned home, no doubt she would be the notorious nobody who'd wrangled the local icon out of an evening.

A few minutes later, Mitch returned with the fluffy cloud of pink sugar on a stick and offered it to her. "Here. It was either this or some weird shade of green."

"This is great."

Tori's first bite of the candy brought back memories of a simpler time. So did the smells of frying funnel cakes and popcorn. Yet everything seemed much more special with Mitch at her side. For the first time, she walked the midway with a man, but not just any man. A special man who so completely tugged at her heartstrings every time he smiled.

"How about we try out a ride?" He snagged a hunk of the cotton candy and popped it into his mouth.

"I don't go for anything too daring," Tori replied. "But I do like the Ferris wheel."

He grinned. "I can't interest you in that kamikaze roller coaster?"

"Not if you value your boots."

"I do, so the Ferris wheel it is."

Again Tori hung back as Mitch purchased tickets from the booth. While waiting their turn to board, they maintained a comfortable silence, Mitch standing behind her with his palms braced on her waist. She resisted the urge to toss the monkey and candy aside to turn into his arms. Definitely not a good idea at the moment. But when they were alone on the ride, she had a good mind to fulfill one of her fantasies, if he proved to be agreeable.

After the wheel executed two go-rounds, their turn finally came. Tori climbed into the red car first and Mitch followed, Lanny positioned between them like a hairy, inanimate child. They pulled the safety bar over their laps and as they ascended backward, Tori's tummy took a pleasant dip. It dipped again when they sat suspended at the top while more riders loaded, providing her with the perfect opportunity to make her request.

Mitch rested his arm along the back of the seat, their thighs touching. That alone made her breathless. She sounded breathless when she said, "Mitch, can I ask you a question?"

He frowned. "I thought maybe we'd forget about the interview tonight."

"This isn't for the article. This is something that I want to know. Off the record."

"Okay."

"Have you ever kissed anyone on a Ferris wheel?"

He took off his hat, ran a hand through his hair, then settled it back on his head. "As best I can recall, I tried that once when I was about thirteen. I got slapped."

Tori twirled the white cone round and round. "I wouldn't slap you."

"You really want me to do that in front of the entire town?"

She kept her eyes focused on the lights spread out before them. "Not if it's going to ruin your rep—"

He stopped her words with a kiss as soft and as sweet as the cotton candy. Even when the ride started moving again, he didn't stop. Tori was barely mindful of the wheel's rotation or the moderate breeze blowing her bangs back from her face. Her awareness centered only on Mitch and the absolute thrill of his mouth moving against hers. He took her hand into his and rubbed her wrist with his thumb in a motion as gentle as the glide of his tongue against hers, as easy as the swaying car.

All too soon, the ride stopped and so did his kiss.

He leaned back against the seat, taking his hand from hers to adjust his hat that had tipped back from his forehead. "That probably melted your candy."

Tori looked down at the said candy to find it gone. "I think it flew away."

Mitch leaned over the side of the car and looked down at the ground below. "Oh, hell. Hope it didn't end up in some matriarch's beehive hairdo."

Tori released a laugh that seemed to float away on the wind along with the last of her heart. "That should make it in the *Quail Run Herald* if our little adolescent display doesn't first."

He patted the monkey's head. "At least you hung on to Lanny."

If only it would be so easy to hang on to Mitch, yet that was as elusive as the whereabouts of the candy. "I guess the earth didn't move just because you kissed me in public."

He regarded her with luminescent blue eyes that gave the

midway lights some serious competition. "I wouldn't necessarily say that."

The wheel jerked forward and soon stopped on the platform, bringing an end to the ride, bringing about Tori's disappointment over the end of a few very memorable moments.

As soon as the attendant lifted the bar, Mitch climbed out and offered his hand for her to take. And he didn't let her go even after they started down the wooden walkway, where they were met with random applause and hoots and hollers from several of the onlookers. Someone shouted, "Way to go, Gus!", prompting Tori to spin around to find Buck standing nearby, a handsome-looking older woman by his side. She sent a quick glance at Mitch to find he didn't look at all pleased at being caught by his grandfather.

Heat rose to Tori's face when she considered the number of people who had played witness to their behavior—particularly the blond bombshell standing near the exit, two furry friends dangling from her hands and two lying on the ground at her feet as she glared at Tori.

As juvenile as it seemed, Tori experienced a strong sense of satisfaction that Mary Alice Marshall had seen poor valedictorian Victoria Barnett in a lip-lock with Mitch Warner. Very petty, but pretty amusing at that.

Again they took to the busy streets, strolling along at a leisurely pace, hand in hand, Lanny clutched tightly in Tori's arm. The magical evening and Mitch's equally magical kiss had taken its toll on Tori. With every whiff of his cologne, every casual touch, she realized how she wanted this evening to end. But not yet. Not until they spent a little more time together. She didn't want to seem too enthusiastic, even if she was.

The masses began to move past them, mothers and fathers and kids, along with assorted couples, young and old, all heading toward Horton's pasture. "The fireworks are about to start in a few minutes," Tori said. "Are you interested in watching?"

Mitch stopped in the middle of the hordes and looked around. "I have a better idea."

Before Tori could inquire about that idea, Mitch turned and tugged her in the opposite direction, against the flow of the crowd. He stopped at the place set up for hayrides provided by a couple of local farmers with tractors and flatbeds. Leaving her behind once more, he spoke briefly with one of the men, handed him what looked to be a few bills, then returned.

He took Tori's arm and said, "Let's go."

A few people had gathered to await their turn, but the farmer waved them away. "This is a private hire, folks. The next ride will be here in about ten minutes."

A collective groan rang out from the bystanders, yet Mitch didn't give them a second glance as he helped Tori onto the trailer covered in hay. They positioned themselves with their backs to the bails lining the perimeter, Lanny between them once more.

The tractor headed out with a spew of fumes and a grating groan, bumping Tori closer to Mitch's side and practically crushing the poor stuffed animal. Some smart kid with a big mouth yelled out, "Give her a hickey," triggering a boom of laughter from those left behind.

"No hickeys," Tori said as she settled closer to him.

He pulled Lanny from between them, tossed him over his shoulder, then wrapped both his arms around her. "Damn. You're going to ruin all my fun tonight."

"You just ruined all of Lanny's fun. Now he's going to get cold."

"Lanny can get his own woman."

"He could borrow a friend from Mary Alice."

Mitch nuzzled his face in her hair. "I don't want to hear her name again, okay?"

"Fine by me. I'd rather concentrate on us having fun."

"That sounds real promising, ma'am." His voice was a rough whisper in her ear. "Here we are again, in the hay under the sky."

Tori trembled but it had nothing to do with the night air because it wasn't that cold. "We didn't have a chaperone the last time we were in this situation."

"And we did have a blanket, which we don't have now."

"I guess that means we should both be on our best behavior."

Mitch scooted down, taking Tori with him and slipped his hand beneath her jacket, bringing it to rest on her rib cage immediately below her breast. "Not necessarily. It's dark out and unless he has night vision, he couldn't see us anyway."

"Mitch Warner, you are a very wicked boy."

He rimmed the shell of her ear with his tongue. "And I can give you a mean hickey."

Tori giggled as he nibbled on her neck. "Don't you dare!"

"Can I at least give you a kiss?"

"Please do."

And he did, only this one wasn't quite as tempered as their Ferris wheel folly. This one was hotter, more insistent, intense. They sank lower and deeper into the hay until they were practically lying down. Their respiration sounded harsh and ragged when they managed to stop for a breath.

Mitch tracked a path with his thumb along the side of her breast, then moved his hand in slow increments until he found and fondled her nipple through the sweater. The snap of fireworks in the distance couldn't compete with the pounding in her ears. The lights flashing in the sky above them had nothing on those sparking behind her eyes when Mitch slid his leg between her legs, rubbing against her in a suggestive rhythm.

When Mitch broke the kiss to slide his tongue down her neck, a needy sound escaped Tori's parted lips. "How much longer is this ride going to go on?" she murmured.

Mitch lifted his head. "Not long enough. He turned around about five minutes ago."

"I didn't notice."

She definitely noticed when Mitch curled his palm on the inside of her thigh where their legs met. "I can't be just your friend, Tori, when I want to make love to you so bad, I physically hurt."

Tori, the former good girl, guided his hand between her

legs, letting him know exactly what she needed and where. "I want to be your friend, Mitch. But I also want to be your lover, at least tonight."

"And tomorrow night and the next, until you have to leave," he said as he plied her with heavenly strokes through the denim of her jeans. "But we can't do this here and do it right."

Tori was on the verge of going over the edge again until Mitch pulled his hand away and shifted them into a sitting position. "Luckily, we're almost there."

"Yes, I was. For the second time today."

He kissed her soundly one more time. "I'll damn sure finish this, baby, if you're sure that's what you really want."

"It is."

"Then let's get off this ride and go home."

Mitch rode all the way home with his hand on Tori's thigh while Bob, who'd had a few too many beers, talked incessantly in the back of the company's extended-cab truck and Stella kept telling him to stuff a sock in it or he wouldn't get any when they got home. Bobby responded by telling Stella they didn't have to wait until they got home, then the smacking kisses and giggles commenced.

By the time they pulled up the drive and deposited the uninhibited couple at their house, Mitch was so on edge he thought his skin might crawl off his body. And worse, the ape stared at him from his seat on the dash, looking as if he might open his monkey mouth and chastise Mitch for his inability to control himself enough to keep his erection reined in until he got Tori alone.

He waited until he saw Bob and Stella close the front door before he turned all that edginess on Tori with a down and dirty kiss, brief but to the point. Then he sped up the drive to his own home, spewing dirt as he braked harder than he'd intended. He yanked open his door, intending to help Tori out but she met him at the hood of the truck. They kissed hot and heavy again before he took her hand and led her inside the foyer, where he claimed her mouth one more time.

He couldn't remember the last time he'd kissed a woman so much in one night. He also couldn't recall when he'd enjoyed kissing a woman this much. Probably never. But kissing wasn't all that was on his mind at the moment, the reason why he tore himself away from Tori's tempting mouth, clasped her hand and led her down the hall faster than he should.

"What about Buck?" Tori asked when they entered his bedroom, her voice little more than a breathless whisper.

Mitch closed the door and tripped the lock. "I really don't give a damn where he is, as long as he isn't in here with us." Although from the looks of things at the fair tonight, his grandfather might be getting lucky, too.

When he turned to Tori, she brushed away her windblown hair, her face flushed. "We left Lanny in the truck," she said.

He approached her slowly. "And that's where he's going to stay. I don't want anything between us." He took two more steps until he stood immediately before her. "No stuffed animals. No clothes. And no apologies for what we're about to do."

"Definitely no apologies, if you continue to live up to the hype."

"I guess you'll know soon enough."

Time seemed to suspend in that moment, the tension so thick Mitch could cut it with his pocketknife. Tori put an end to the hesitation by tugging his shirt from his waistband, tearing at the snaps and peeling it off his shoulders.

Clasping the hem of her black sweater, he lifted it over her head and tossed it aside. Her hair was even more mussed now and she looked sexy as hell standing there in a scrap of a black lace bra that barely concealed her breasts. Mitch didn't attempt to remove that because she beat him to the punch. And what a punch he received when she shrugged it off, revealing tawny nipples drawn tight. He'd never had the pleasure to inspect them in the light until now, but that inspection was short lived when Tori dove for his buckle and popped it and the button on his fly open.

Determined to slow down and savor the moment, Mitch

gathered her up into his arms and laid her on the bed. He sat on the edge of the mattress and worked her jeans down her legs, tossing them aside to join her clothes on the floor, leaving her clad in only a scrap of black satin. Although his own jeans were as tight as a vise, he chose to remain dressed for the time being and simply study her for a few moments, with his eyes and hands.

"You're so damn beautiful." When he brushed his knuckles over her abdomen below her navel, she began to tremble, from her belly to her legs.

Concerned, Mitch glanced up to see that her eyes were tightly closed. He leaned over, his arms on either side of her. "Tori, are you okay with this?"

She opened her eyes and sent him a slight smile. "I'm very okay with it."

"You're shaking."

"I can't help it. I'm excited."

"Are you sure? Because we can stop if you—"

"Mitch, if you stop now, I'll never forgive you."

He traced her lips with the tip of his tongue. "I couldn't have you holding a grudge, now could I?"

"Precisely. Now take off your clothes and let's get on with it."

"Not yet," he said. "Not until I get a good look at you."

He bracketed her pelvis between his hands and rubbed downward with his thumbs, performing an impromptu massage as he lowered her panties. When he had them resting at the tops of her thighs, he lifted her bottom and pulled them completely away.

For a man who needed to be inside her more than he needed air, the pace had been agonizingly slow, but well worth the time it had taken. He didn't intend to pick up speed, not until he had her exactly where he wanted her to be.

"Open your legs for me, babe," he told her, using his palms to encourage her. "And don't close your eyes."

Her uneven breathing told him she was wound tight, and so

was Mitch, to the point of possible combustion. But that possibility didn't stop him from taking his time as he slid his fingers through the soft cloud of curls, remaining there to play for a few moments before seeking her slick, warm flesh. She was so primed for his touch that he knew it would take no time at all for her to climax. For that reason, he tempered his strokes, alternating between watching her face and watching the movement of his hand as he explored her, both inside and out.

Her respiration increased and her body tightened around his fingers as the first signs of orgasm overtook her. He wanted to replace his hand with his mouth, but she was already too far gone. Instead, he kissed her until every last ripple of the release subsided. Now he could join her in that state of oblivion.

He pushed away from her and stood at the side of the bed, fumbling for his zipper in harried anticipation.

"Mitch." He looked up to see Tori seated on the edge of the mattress where he had been. "Come here," she said, her voice much calmer now, as if she had regained her control where Mitch had done anything but.

He walked to her and watched as she lowered his fly, then did the same with his jeans and briefs. After he shrugged out of them completely, she held out her arms and, with only a look, invited him inside. But before he could join her, he still had something else to consider. Something he'd vowed not to forget again.

Pulling open the nightstand drawer, he withdrew a gold foil packet and held it up. "Should I use this?"

She failed to look at him as she tossed back the quilt and slid beneath the sheet. "I think that's a good idea, just to be on the safe side."

Her tone, her hesitant gaze, sent a sliver of apprehension up Mitch's spine. Maybe the other night she hadn't been honest with him. Maybe they had taken a huge risk. Yet as he studied her lying there in his bed, her skin flushed and her eyes wide, his desperate need for her outweighed any concerns over what might have been. He only wanted what could be. What would be.

After rolling on the condom, he snapped off the lamp and tossed back the sheet to take his place beside Tori. The three-quarter moon filtering in from the open curtains cast her face in muted light, her eyes as dark as the night.

Holding her face in his palms, he took another moment to just look at her. "I've wanted you non-stop since we were together in the truck. You've had me on a slow burn for four days. Every time I think about you, I get hard."

"Hard is good."

"Not when you're riding a horse. When I saw you standing outside the arena today, talking to Buck, it was all I could do not to tell the boys to go away, toss you over my shoulder and take you to this bed."

"And I might have let you."

"Oh, yeah?"

"Yes, even though my original goal was strictly friendship."

His only goal at the moment was to please her. To make her feel so good she wouldn't consider being anywhere else but his bed for the time they had left. "Tell me what you want, Tori. I'll do anything you want me to do."

With her hands on his hips, she encouraged him to move over her. "I want you inside of me. I want it deep. I want it hard."

Nearing the point of madness, Mitch reached between them and guided himself inside her, pausing before he was completely immersed in her heat. "How deep?" he asked, inching in a little more.

"I want to feel all of you."

He moved a little more. "How's this?"

"Is that the best you can do?" Her voice was low and throaty, enticing as hell, driving Mitch to the brink.

With one hard thrust, he seated himself completely and nearly came undone in the process. "Better?" That one-word question took a lot of effort and so did his determination to hold on a little longer.

She slid her fingers through his hair and moved her hips beneath him. "The best."

He wanted to be the best she'd ever had.

With all the strength he could muster, he reached over and grabbed the other pillow then pulled her up to prop it on top of the pillow already positioned beneath her shoulders. Then he lifted her bottom in his palms and drove into her.

Even if he'd wanted to slow it down, he couldn't. Not with her welcoming this wild, unrestrained rhythm resulting from all the desire they'd held for each other from the moment they'd met. Not when she kissed him, her tongue meeting his in time with their thrusts and her nails raking down his back. Not when he felt the first contractions of her climax pulling him even deeper still.

His heart pounded against his chest as the pressure built and built, then exploded, fast and furious. He rode the waves with Tori in his arms, his face buried in the softness of her neck, his body jolted from the intensity of the climax.

In the aftermath, they were now covered in sweat, surrounded by the heady scent of sex and finally calmed by the long-awaited satisfaction. Or at least Tori seemed calm. Now Mitch was the one who was shaking.

Tori lifted his head in her hands and stared at him. "Are *you* okay?"

"If I were any better, I'd be dead." He rolled to his side, taking her with him. "I don't want you to leave."

The words jumped out before he'd even had time to register exactly what he was saying.

"I wouldn't want Buck to know I'm in your bed," she said, obviously misunderstanding his meaning. He thought it best not to enlighten her, at least not until he analyzed why he hated the thought of her returning home. Right now, he had to keep her beside him all night.

He kissed her softly and rubbed her shoulder. "Buck might not be in until morning. And even if he's here right now, he doesn't know where you are. Stay with me tonight. All night."

She settled her cheek against his chest. "Okay. I'll stay tonight."

That promise seemed inadequate to Mitch because he

wanted more than tonight with her. He recognized some sort of transformation was occurring inside him. He damn sure didn't know what to do about that, or why Tori Barnett was making him feel things he'd never felt, never wanted to feel.

But he did know that as long as he had this lady in his arms, he was going to enjoy it. Tomorrow, he'd think about the rest.

Two hours later, Tori sat in the small chair positioned in front of the picture window in Mitch's bedroom, hugging her legs to her chest as she stared into the night. She wore his discarded shirt, the only thing she could locate in the darkened room. The fabric held the trace scent of his cologne, and so did her body.

The moon looked hazy, but then that might have to do with her unexpected tears. She could chalk up the irrational emotions to hormones. Or she could go ahead and admit that her current state resulted from the realization that she was falling in love with Mitch Warner.

She had never intended to do such an inadvisable thing, but her mind had been a giant jumble since the first time she'd danced with him. So had her heart.

She recalled when he had graced the pages of tabloids and teen magazines, an enigmatic young man who'd captured nationwide attention with his looks alone. He'd been born into wealth and a political legacy, a favorite pick to fashion the nation's future—smart, handsome and eligible.

At that particular time, Tori's interest in Mitch had been limited to the news coverage, due to her first thoughts of becoming a journalist, not desire for him or his kind—a typical, spoiled rich kid who'd had the world handed to him while she'd had to struggle for everything she'd obtained. She also remembered viewing one photo immediately after he'd been accepted to Harvard and another when he'd been caught on film escorting a beautiful co-ed to a college formal. But she'd never really seen him smile. She'd believed him to be arrogant, that he'd thought himself above showing any true emotion.

Now she recognized that she'd seen sadness in those magnetic blue eyes, not snobbery or self-absorption. And if all those women who'd fantasized about him really knew the man beneath the façade, as Tori now did, they would have worshipped him even more.

Still, she and Mitch hailed from different societal positions. They had very different aspirations. She longed for a successful career and recognition for her efforts. He yearned for obscurity and a normal life.

And she was beginning to feel guilty that in some ways she had been using him to attain that success and security. But she had to rationalize that she could assist him in maintaining his privacy by stressing that he wanted to be left alone. They both would win in the end.

Except Tori would suffer a loss in exchange for that success when she left him behind.

For that reason, she needed to start viewing this liaison exactly as it was—nothing more than a brief affair between two consenting adults. She needed to shore up her emotions, beginning now.

Standing, she turned and took one last look at Mitch. He slept on his side facing the window, the sheet draped carelessly over his hips, exposing only the tops of his thighs and the flat plane of his belly, his arms tucked beneath the pillow, his eyes closed against the limited light of the moon and Tori's scrutiny.

She wanted desperately to climb back beneath the covers and mold herself to his strong back. She wanted to wake him one more time and fuel the fire between them with a few touches. Instead, she bypassed the bed and headed out the door, leaving her discarded clothes, and Mitch, behind.

Tori needed time to think and assess. She needed to sleep. She couldn't do either with him so close.

Tomorrow, she would continue the interview process. If more intimacy occurred between them, she would strive to keep her feelings out of it. She would take what he had to offer, engage in a little self-discovery and enjoy their remaining time together without inhibition.

A solid plan. A good plan. Now she just had to stick to it.

Eight

Mitch had hated waking at dawn to find Tori gone. He'd had every intention of making love to her again before they started their day. At breakfast, he'd planned to confront her over the disappearing act but she hadn't shown up. When he'd gone to her room to seek her out, he'd found her bed made and the place totally deserted. As irrational as it seemed, he'd worried she'd taken the first plane back to Dallas after last night. It wasn't until Bob had told him Tori was up at the old house with Stella that he'd allowed himself to relax—as much as a man with an illogical need for a woman could relax.

After he accomplished something constructive, Mitch planned to let her know that he wanted her in his bed until she left on Sunday, no argument. If she appeared reluctant, he'd just have to find a way to convince her, and he could think of a lot of ways.

That brought about a smile as he sat at his desk, checking the status of pending software shipments. He wasn't having a whole lot of luck concentrating on his business when the business of making love to Tori was still so fresh on his mind. His concentration went completely by the wayside when the knock came at the door followed by, "Mitch, can I come in?"

"Door's open," he replied as he braced himself for the impact of seeing Tori again, as if he could prepare. Just hearing her voice had him on edge.

Tori entered the room dressed in a navy blazer and a skirt that hit just above her knees, revealing her legs and a pair of matching moderate high heels. Her straight brown hair flowed over her shoulders, stopping where the collar formed a V above her breasts. The suit was business conservative, tasteful, but to Mitch, she might as well have been wearing nothing at all, considering the impact on his libido.

Mitch leaned back in his chair. "Where have you been?"

She hooked a thumb over her shoulder. "Actually, I've been talking to some of the hands. I wanted to ask them a few questions."

"And you did it dressed like that?" His tone sounded gruff and jealous. He'd be damned if he wasn't.

Tori smoothed a hand down the skirt. "They didn't seem to mind."

"I'm sure they didn't mind at all. In fact, you probably made their day, showing up in that outfit."

"I meant they didn't seem to notice."

Mitch tented his fingers beneath his chin. "I never pegged you as being that naïve, Tori. They're men. They noticed. Especially Rand. He might seem like the quiet type, but you have to be careful around him."

As if bent on ignoring him, she slid the black bag off her shoulder and set it down on the sofa then pulled out a yellow notepad. "I have some interesting comments here. The overall opinion is you're fair and generous. One man said that he, and I quote, 'considers you a good friend, second only to his bluetick hound.' The only real criticism came when Rand said you're not always pleasant if you haven't had your coffee. Have you had your coffee today, Mitch?"

"Are you saying I'm not pleasant enough for you?"

"You are a little testy." She went back to the notes. "However, I am happy to report that the general consensus is that you're a generous employer and a good man."

When she swept her hair away from her shoulder and smiled, Mitch had the strongest urge to show her exactly how good he could be. "I still don't understand why it was necessary to get all dressed up to talk to the help."

"I'm dressed up because I plan to go into town with Stella. She wants to shop for some fabric for the nursery curtains. While I'm there, I'll interview a few people to give the story some local color. In order to do that, I need to appear professional."

Did she have to look so sexy doing it? "Fine. I'm sure they won't tell you all that much."

"I'll take my chances, but first...." Rifling in the bag, she exchanged the pad for a camera and waved it at him. "Picture time. I want to show you in your element. The cowboy working at the computer." She lifted the camera and said, "Smile."

Mitch didn't feel like smiling. The only thing he wanted to do right now was make her smile, utilizing his hands and mouth. To appease her, he sent her a halfway grin. She seemed satisfied and snapped the camera, nearly blinding Mitch with the flash.

"Great," she said. "One more."

She didn't wait for a smile or for Mitch's vision to return before she took two more shots.

"Enough," Mitch said. "I can't see a thing." That wouldn't do at all since he didn't want to miss a minute of seeing her, especially in that suit.

"Sorry," she said. "That's enough for now."

Not by a long shot, Mitch decided. He moved from behind his desk and held out his hand. "Give it here. I want to take a couple of pictures of you."

"Me?"

"Yeah. I want a souvenir."

She laid a dramatic hand above her breasts. “Well, if I must. Where do you want me?”

He grinned. “Honestly?”

She frowned. “For the picture, Mitch.”

Stepping aside, he gestured toward his desk. “Sit there.”

“You want me on the desk?”

Oh, yeah. That was a fine idea. “We could do it on the sofa, but I think the desk adds a unique perspective.”

“If you say so.” Finally she complied, hoisting herself up with her palms, her legs dangling and her hands folded primly in her lap.

Mitch didn’t want prim and proper. “Cross your legs and pull the hem of your skirt up a little. Show me some leg.”

She complied and leaned back on her palms, then topped off the pose with a coy look. “How’s this?”

Pretty damn good, but he wanted to see a little more skin. If he had to settle for a picture as a replacement after she left, he wanted a good one. “Unbutton the top button on your jacket.”

“Mitch—”

“Just do it, Tori. You might actually enjoy it.” He sure was, and he’d only just begun.

Tori got the button undone after a couple of attempts. Mitch suspected she was nervous, but he also wondered if maybe she was a little turned on by it all. He planned to find that out, real soon. Stepping back, he snapped a picture then narrowed his eyes. “Open your jacket up a little.”

“If I do that, you’ll be able to see my bra.”

“I know.”

She drew in a shaky breath and released it slowly. “Why, Mitch Warner, I didn’t know you were serious about taking naughty pictures.”

“Sexy pictures, Tori. Just a little suggestive.”

“Oh, so you want suggestive, do you?” she said, challenge in her tone and her dark eyes.

She released every last one of the jacket buttons and opened it completely, exposing her navy satin bra and shocking the hell out of Mitch in the process. She shook her head, mussing her hair so that it now looked as untamed as Mitch felt. And when she inched her skirt up to the tops of her thighs, he reclaimed enough coherency to back up and lock the door.

"Is this suggestive enough?" she asked when he stepped forward.

"Oh, yeah. That looks real good."

When he continued to stand there, greatly enjoying the sight, Tori asked, "Are you going to take the picture?"

He didn't want another picture. He wanted her. Now.

After tossing the camera into the bag, he strode to his desk and moved in front of her. Her skin was flushed, either from self-consciousness or excitement. He hoped it was the latter. Hoped that she was experiencing the steady burn she'd incited in him.

Mitch pulled her up from the desk and into his arms, wrapping her legs around his waist as he carried her to the sofa and deposited her there. He leaned over to kiss her, deep, hard, unrelenting, before he worked the jacket off her slender shoulders and pulled her arms from the sleeves. He trailed his lips down her neck, pausing to slide his tongue along the edging of her bra. When he heard her gasp, he raised his head and found her staring at him with anticipation.

"This morning, I didn't like finding you gone from my bed," he told her as he played with her nipples through the bra.

"I thought it might be better if I slept in my own bed, in case Buck should become suspicious."

"I don't care what Buck thinks. I just want to make you feel as good as you made me felt last night. Let me do that, Tori."

"What if someone wants you?"

"I want you, and that's all that matters."

Her sigh echoed in the room. "Mitch, you're making it hard for me to be a good girl."

"Tori, you're just making me hard."

Mitch crouched before her and propped both her legs on his

shoulder. He removed her shoes, one at a time, before reaching beneath her skirt to tug her panties up her legs slowly, then lifted her heels to completely pull them away.

Tori stared at Mitch, mute, the rasp of her respiration the only sound disturbing the quiet. The power of his gaze, the soft strokes he breezed up and down her thighs with his callused palms, the anticipation, robbed her of any desire to protest anything he might attempt.

For a fleeting moment, she questioned his goal when he lifted her bottom and pushed her skirt up until it bunched below her waist. All doubt dissolved, and so did she, when he dropped to his knees, nudged her legs apart with his shoulders and lowered his head.

Tori wasn't exactly a novice when it came to sex, definitely not a schoolgirl virgin. She had knowledge of the ways a man and woman could express themselves during lovemaking, but mostly through girl talk, not through practice.

The gentle sweep of Mitch's tongue, the unyielding tug of his lips, the caress of his fingertips went beyond her realm of experience. Beyond anything she had ever known before with a man, even her former lover.

The tempting taboo of it all sent her into an abyss where nothing existed except pure feeling. Her head listed to one side as Mitch continued to assail her, using his mouth as a lovely weapon to daze and weaken her, leaving her helpless to do anything but stare in wonderment.

When the climax claimed her, she tried to prolong it with every last bit of her strength. But she didn't have the will to stop it any more than she had the will to stop Mitch from keeping her captive with his mouth.

As Tori drifted back to reality and her heartbeat began to slow, she tipped her head back and closed her eyes, only mildly aware of the rasp of a zipper and the rattle of paper. She recognized then that Mitch was not quite done with her yet, and she wasn't quite sure she could handle more of his sensual torture.

But she was darn sure going try, she thought when he said, "Come here, Tori," in a low, controlled voice

She opened her eyes to see his jeans pushed to his knees, his shirttail doing little to conceal his erection. Like a boneless puppet, she didn't resist when he clasped her waist and directed her onto his lap to straddle his thighs. While she watched, he released the buttons on his shirt, allowing it to fall open.

Keeping his eyes locked on hers, Mitch lifted her up and guided her to his erection. Now it was Tori's turn to level her own brand of torture on him. She moved her hips in a slow, teasing rhythm, taking him inside her in small increments. She watched his face as she quickened the tempo, his jaw clenched tight. The power she experienced was a little hedonistic, and well-deserved considering the power he'd held over her. She bent to kiss him, nipping at his lips as she moved in a wilder cadence. A groan escaped his lips and she leaned back, knowing that in a matter of moments, he would be exactly where she had been minutes before, where she was going again because of Mitch's touch.

This release hit her as hard as the first, sending shock waves through her body as she took Mitch completely inside. A long breath hissed out of his mouth and she felt the steady pulse of his climax.

Tori collapsed against his bare chest, her palms curled over his solid shoulders as if she needed to hang on for dear life, her cheek resting over his strong heart. For such a reckless ride into oblivion, she felt incredibly content.

After a time, Mitch pressed a kiss to her temple and said, "I could get used to this."

So could she, and that was dangerous. "Guess there's something to be said for having outrageous sex in an office."

"It's not just the lovemaking, Tori. I could get used to having you around for more than a few days."

She raised her head and met his solemn gaze. "Unfortunately, I have to go back to work."

He brushed her hair away from her shoulders. "I know, but I want to see you again after that."

A tiny glimmer of hope radiated from Tori's heart. "That might be difficult since I live in Dallas and you live here."

"Maybe we could work something out."

"I'm open to suggestions."

He brushed a kiss across her lips. "Here's a good suggestion. I want you in my bed until you leave. We'll discuss the rest later."

That sounded more like a demand than a suggestion, but she didn't have the strength or desire to refuse. "Okay, but what about Buck?"

He grinned. "Three's a crowd."

She playfully slapped at his arm. "You know what I mean. I wouldn't want him to think badly of me."

"Don't worry about Buck. He always minds his own business."

"I know it's none of my business, but you're heading for trouble."

Seated at the dinette in the kitchen, Mitch looked up from his beer and glared at his grandfather. "What are you talking about?"

Buck turned a chair around, straddled it and rested his arms on the back. "You're stringing that girl along, and I don't like it one damn bit."

Mitch scratched at the label with a thumbnail. "In case you haven't noticed, we're both adults and well above the legal age."

"I know that. I also know that she's got feelings for you and I don't want to see them trampled."

"I don't intend to do that."

"What you intend to do and what you will do are two different things."

Mitch continued to stare at the brown bottle, dotted with condensation that was no match for the beads of sweat on his forehead. "What makes you think I'm going to hurt her?"

"Have you asked her to marry you?"

That garnered Mitch's full attention. "No."

"Why not?"

Mitch felt as if he were being reprimanded for staying out past curfew, only this was a much more serious offense, apparent by Buck's tone. "One, we barely know each other. Two, I have no plans to marry anyone and you know that."

Buck tipped his straw hat back from his brow. "Maybe you need to reconsider what you're doing by keeping her in your bed. Tori's a nice girl and she deserves a man who isn't gun-shy when it comes to matrimony."

"You're getting way ahead of the game, Buck. She's got a career that's important to her. As far as I know, she's not interested in anything too serious, either."

"Are you sure?"

Tori didn't strike him as being the kind who wanted a husband and babies, but he'd been wrong about women before. "Tell you what. If you'll stop grilling me about the women in my life, then I won't ask where you've been the past few nights."

"I've been with Eula Jenkins if you hafta know."

"You've been bedding the town's most proper widow?" Mitch shook his head. "Talk about trouble."

Buck snorted. "We're both a little long in the tooth for you to be passing judgment."

Mitch couldn't resist turning the tables on Buck. "Tell me something. Are you going to marry her?"

"Stranger things have happened. And you'll be the last to know if I propose."

Mitch barked out a laugh. "That'll be the day, you getting married again."

"It's a lot more possible than you going to the altar." Buck rubbed a gnarled hand across his stubbled chin. "Just a little more advice, Gus. One of these days you're going to have to let go of your anger over your daddy remarrying or it's going to eat you up inside and ruin your chance at being happy."

Mitch didn't think he would ever get over the betrayal, and he resented his grandfather for shoving it back in his face. "Don't you have something to do?"

Buck climbed from the chair with more agility than many twenty-year-olds. "Yeah. I gotta go get on the Internet. My chat buddies are expectin' me."

"Have a good time."

"I will. And you have a care because if you break that little girl's heart, you're going to hear it from me."

As Buck strode away, Mitch took a swig of his beer and set it down hard on the table. Maybe his grandfather was making some sense. Maybe he should just let it be over after Tori left.

But deep down, he couldn't stomach the thought of letting her walk away without ever seeing her again. He'd just have to take that out and think about it later. Right now, he needed to get some work done.

At least Tori had accomplished something besides having a little afternoon delight with Mitch Warner. She'd talked to several of the town's more prosperous citizens, including the owner of the feed store, who'd been highly complimentary about Mitch's community involvement, and Betty Galloway, the city secretary, who'd been forthright about Mitch's commitment to the local school through his elected position on the board. Obviously he wasn't so averse to politics after all, something Tori found somewhat amusing.

Mentally and physically exhausted, Tori now sat in the corner booth of Moore's Drug and Soda Fountain—the business that had been in Stella's family for sixty years—waiting for her best friend to finish up at the grocer's so they could head back to the ranch. Her thoughts continuously kept drifting back to the interlude in Mitch's office, and his declaration that he wanted to see her again after she returned home. Maybe they could try it for a while. And maybe their relationship might progress into something solid. A girl could always play at optimism.

Tori sipped at her cherry cola and almost choked when she heard the familiar feminine voice coming from the counter to her right. Her gaze zipped to the leggy blonde chatting away about the new house with Gracie, the waitress who'd worked at the fountain since Moses was in knickers.

She wanted to slink down in the booth to avoid another confrontation with Mary Alice but instead remained upright, pretending to look out the window at the limited traffic on Main Street.

"Is this seat taken?"

Tori cursed Stella's tardiness as she stared up at Mary Alice. "I'm expecting someone."

"Mitch?"

It would be too easy for Tori to lie but she opted for the truth. "Actually, Stella. She should be along any time now."

Mary Alice slid into the booth across from Tori and rested her cheeks in her palms. "I'll leave when she gets here, but first, I just wanted to say that you're the talk of the town."

Tori internally cringed. "How so?"

"It's my understanding your doing some sort of story on Mitch. Is it true?"

Relief relaxed Tori's stiff shoulders. "Yes, I am."

"Is this for a newspaper?"

"It's for a magazine."

Mary Alice sat back and folded her arms across her middle. "Oh. One of those grocery store rags?"

Tori quelled the urge to wipe the smug look off the bimbo's face. "It's a monthly magazine and very reputable. We do features on prominent Texas businesswomen. Every now and then, we cover successful men, the reason why I'm interviewing Mitch."

"Tell me something. Is making out with those men part of the interview process?"

Stay calm, Victoria. "That was just a friendly kiss. Spontaneous. It didn't mean anything." A whopper of a lie. It had meant everything.

"I take it this job of yours pays well?"

"It's a great job."

"I guess you live in one of those posh downtown apartments."

"It's a nice apartment." A small one bedroom apartment that happened to be in a Dallas suburb, the only thing she could afford until she paid off the medical bills, a fact Mary Alice did not need to know.

Tori was surprised that Mary Alice actually looked interested, and wistful, when she continued her queries. "Is there a lot going on in Dallas? I mean, do you go to museums and that sort of thing?"

"Sure. When I have time. Dallas has great opportunities in terms of culture. Haven't you ever been there?"

Mary Alice frowned. "Once, a long time ago. I considered moving to Houston to go to college right after high school."

"Why didn't you?"

"Well, because Daddy…" Her gaze faltered. "Because I decided to go to the community college in Halbert County. I studied business so I could help Daddy out at the mill."

Tori wasn't buying any of her bull. "You could have done that in Houston."

She presented a fake smile. "I like living in Quail Run, close to my family."

As unlikely as it seemed, Tori actually felt sorry for her. "It's never too late, Mary Alice. There's a whole wide world out there. You shouldn't settle."

Mary Alice looked totally incensed. "I'm not settling. I'm going to marry Brady and have a nice life."

"I'm sure you will," Tori said, unconvinced that Mary Alice believed her own shtick. "But if you're having second thoughts, it's best to stop now before you find yourself stuck in a marriage you don't really want."

Mary Alice slid from the booth, this time more quickly than she'd entered, her expression stony with anger. "Thanks for the advice, Tori. Now let me give you some about Mitch."

"I don't need any advice about Mitch."

Ignoring Tori's protest, Mary Alice set a palm on the table and leaned into it. "Has he taken you down to the creek yet? That's his favorite place to make love."

"I assure you we have not been to the creek."

"But you have been in his bed."

Tori wondered if she had guilt scribbled all over her face. "What makes you think something intimate's going on between us?"

"Because Mitch Warner is a hypnotist, especially when it comes to sex. He's good at everything he does, and he's great at giving a woman what she needs, although I'm betting you already know that."

This time Tori looked away. "Mitch is only a friend."

"I hope that's true, otherwise you'll spend nine years of your life trying to convince him to settle down. He won't do it, Tori. He's not the marrying kind so you can get that out of your head."

"I don't have that in my head."

"Good, because he's a lost cause when it comes to commitment. I found that out the hard way."

The sadness in Mary Alice's voice drew Tori's gaze to her melancholy expression. "You're still in love with him, aren't you?"

"Sure. He's very easy to love. But I guess you know that. And if you don't now, you will."

With that, Mary Alice walked away, leaving Tori alone with food for thought and shattered hope. She knew all too well that the advice Mitch's former lover had bestowed on her was good counsel.

It would be best to think of Mitch as only her friend and nothing more. She would physically accept what he offered for the rest of the week, then she would walk away while her heart was still relatively undamaged. Before she agreed to be his good-time good girl with no future in the offing.

For the first time in ten years, Mitch had failed to attend the annual rodeo. Instead, he'd opted to spend the night with Tori—the night before she returned to Dallas, leaving him behind.

As far as he was concerned, the week had passed too fast,

although he couldn't complain about the time they'd spent together, especially when they'd made love. And they'd made love a whole lot, at night and in the morning in his bed. During the day, in his office or behind the hay in the barn. She'd been willing to experiment, to try new positions, and they'd mastered quite a few. The only thing she'd refused was his offer to make love at his favorite fishing spot down by the creek.

Right now she sat on the sofa in the den across from him, wearing only his shirt at his request, her feet propped in his lap so he could give them a rubdown. He planned to give her a rubdown all over her body as soon as she quit asking all the damn questions.

She flipped through her notes, then tucked the pen behind her ear and set the pad down beside her. "Okay, I have about everything I need here except for one thing. I need some sort of quote about your father."

Mitch paused with his hand on her instep. "I told you I don't want to talk about him beyond the fact that I don't want to inherit his kingdom."

"Can't you think of anything nice to say about him?"

"I respect his abilities as a national leader."

"That's a start."

"That's the end of it, Tori. I'm not budging on this issue."

She slid her feet off his lap and scooted forward on the sofa, studying him with intense dark eyes. "Do you want to say anything about your mother?"

If he listed all her good points, that would take an entire page, maybe two. "She was a great lady and much more than my father deserved."

Tori slid the pencil from behind her ear and tapped it on the pad before gripping it in both hands. "A few nights ago, I went into the den while you were sleeping to do some more research on the computer. From everything I've read, it seems your parents were very much in love."

Although Mitch had never understood it, his mother had adored his father right to the end. "Don't believe everything you read."

"I don't, but I've seen pictures of them together. Stories that talked about how they were inseparable before she became ill. Are you telling me that wasn't the case?"

Mitch forked a hand through his hair. "When she was sick, he didn't have time for her. In fact, he wasn't even there when..." He let the declaration fade away because he didn't want to get into that with Tori. Resurrecting those old memories, the bitterness, wouldn't bode well for their last night together. And it could be their last night if he didn't convince her to see him in the future, a subject she hadn't wanted to broach to this point.

She leaned forward and touched his knee. "Are you telling me your father wasn't there when your mother died?"

"I don't want to talk about it."

"I think you need to talk about it. Maybe you'll feel better."

He attempted a forced smile. "The only thing that would make me feel better is if you take off that shirt and come sit in my lap."

"No you don't," she said. "No sexy talk. Not until you answer my question."

Fueled by his sudden anger, Mitch bolted from the chair and began to pace. "Okay, Tori, if you really want the truth, I'll tell you. But it's ugly."

"I can handle it."

He braced one arm on a bookshelf, determined not to look at her, otherwise he might not get this out. "My mother wanted to die at home, and she considered the ranch home, not the Bellaire mansion my father bought to impress all his cronies. So I made the arrangements for her to travel here by ambulance, against my father's wishes. He was royally pissed at me for doing it."

"And he wasn't at her side for that reason?"

"He was here the morning she died, but he had to get back to D.C. to do the nation's business."

"He left knowing she was going to die?"

Mitch hated to admit the truth, but he felt it only fair to do so. "We didn't know it was going to be that day exactly, but we knew she was close. He should've stayed anyway."

"Were you with her when she died?"

"Yeah." This was the most difficult part—the memories of his mother going to sleep and never waking up while he watched. "She slipped into a coma that afternoon while I was reading to her from this." He pulled out the book of poetry. "She revered John Donne. She taught me to appreciate poetry."

Sadness turned her dark eyes even darker. "I did something similar the day my mother died."

"You read to her?"

"I sang to her."

Mitch wasn't at all surprised, and he could imagine how much that had meant to her mother. "What did you sing?"

"The same song I sang the night we met. She loved Patsy Cline. I think that particular song had to do with her feelings for my father, although we never discussed that. It seemed to hurt her to talk about him."

"Where is your father now?"

"I don't know. In fact, I don't even know his name because I never asked, and my mom never offered. She did give me an envelope on my sixteenth birthday that contained his identity. I've never opened it."

Mitch had erroneously assumed that she didn't see her dad by choice. He'd never begun to consider she hadn't met him. "Why haven't you tried to find out more about him?"

"Maybe I just want to keep hanging on to the resentment. I guess we're alike in that respect, resenting our fathers because of what they have or haven't done. But at least you had a father to lean on after your mom was gone."

"Buck, yeah. My dad, no." Mitch shoved the book back into place and faced Tori. "Then the bastard had the nerve to remarry six months later."

Tori's confusion was apparent in her expression. "I thought he remarried a year later."

"That's what he wanted everyone to believe, and he had the

means to cover it up. That whole wedding the following year was only a show for the media. He betrayed my mother's memory and he came out of it without suffering a scratch on his well-regarded record."

"Do you think he was seeing your stepmother before your mother's death?"

"He denied it to me. But I've never believed it."

Tori rose from the sofa and laid a hand on his shoulder. "Sometimes things happen between people that are beyond control, especially when it comes to grief. Maybe he's telling the truth."

Mitch shook off her hand and turned his back to her again. He expected her to listen, to understand, not to side with his father. "It's not important anymore. That was a long time ago. I don't care to rehash it, so let's drop it."

"I understand. You're not willing to forgive your father. But at least you have one, even if he isn't perfect. That's more than I've ever had."

Remorse for his insensitivity turned Mitch toward Tori again, only to find she was at the door. "Where are you going?"

"To bed."

"I'll be there in a while."

She finally faced him. "To *my* bed, Mitch. I think you need some time alone tonight. And I'm sorry if I've made you dredge up some painful memories. I was only trying to help."

She had helped him in many ways, if only by listening, that much Mitch acknowledged. But his pride prevented him from protesting, even though he wanted to be with her this last night more than he'd wanted anything in a long, long time. "Fine. If that's what you want."

"I'll see you in the morning," she said, then left without a glance in his direction.

And more than likely, tomorrow morning might very well be the last time he would see her. He couldn't blame her for walking away from his bitterness. He understood why she wouldn't want to be involved with a man who'd made it his goal to steer clear of committing to anything aside from his business. A man who had been so caught up in his own anger that he hadn't even stopped to consider that she'd never known her own father.

Spending the night without her in his arms would be his punishment, and he should just accept it like a man. But he'd be damned if he would.

Nine

Lying on her side facing the window, Tori felt the bend of the mattress behind her and smelled the trace scent of summer-fresh soap. She sensed his heat a second before he settled against her back and his arms came around her.

"I'm sorry, babe," he whispered. "I don't know what else to say."

As far as Tori was concerned, he didn't have to say anything else. Although she believed it unwise to accept his apology so easily, she felt powerless to do anything else. An even trade for spending a last night with him.

Turning into his arms, she buried her face against his bare shoulder. Although he had removed all of his clothes, he simply held her for a long while, as if reluctant to make another move. Or perhaps this was what he needed from her at the moment, someone to absorb the pain and anger that still haunted him like a restless spirit.

Tori did want more from him. She wanted to remember being so closely joined with him that she didn't know where she began and he ended. To remember what it was like to be totally lost in love with a man, something she'd never understood until now.

She breezed her hand down his back, over the curve of his hip and then back up his side before reaching between them to touch him. He was already aroused, even before the first steady stroke of her fingertips. When she continued to explore, a slight groan slipped from his lips before he gave her a meaningful kiss propelled by pent-up emotion and the ever-present passion. He clasped her wrist and brought her hand to his lips for a kiss, then sent his hands over, touching places both innocent and intimate. Rolling her onto her back, he kissed his way down her body, breathing soft sensuous words against her skin, stopping to finesse her breasts then working his warm, wonderful mouth lower, bringing her to the sweetest release she had known in his arms.

He moved over her without a sound, entered her with a sigh, made love to her carefully as if she were precious. Then the passion prevailed, setting them on a frantic course. When they were spent in each others' arms, their skin damp from the heat of the lovemaking, their ragged breathing echoing in the silent room, only then did Tori realize what they'd forgotten. Again.

Although the timing wasn't conducive to pregnancy, she felt she should be honest with him about the chance they'd taken, both tonight and the first night they had been together. Yet when he whispered, "I can't get enough of you," in her ear, she couldn't quite find the strength to tell him. Not yet. But she had to tell him before night's end.

He rolled onto his back and settled her against his chest, stroking her hair and kissing her forehead as he always did in the aftermath, a habit of his she had come to appreciate and cherish. Only one more of the many reasons she loved him, and she did love him, wise or not.

Mitch's rough sigh signaled the end of the comfortable silence. "I've never told anyone about the moments before my mother's death. Not even Buck. He left the room because he couldn't handle it."

Tori found it odd that Mitch hadn't blamed Buck for his absence where he had blamed his dad. She also suspected that he was concerned she might use that information in the article. "I promise it will stay between you and me."

"And if you ever decide to find your father, I have a few connections who could probably help."

"I really appreciate that, Mitch." And she did. "But I'll only consider doing that when I decide to have children. I would want to have a medical history, if that's possible. I doubt I would pursue any kind of relationship with him, and that's assuming he would even want that."

"You plan to have kids?" His incredulous tone cut Tori to the quick.

"In the future." Quite possibly in the near future, if she'd become pregnant that first night they were together. It was now or never. "Speaking of children, there's something I need to tell you."

He tensed against her side. "You already have a kid?"

"No. The birth control shot I told you about, well, it's been a while since I had it. It might not be effective. I don't think there's a huge chance I could be pregnant, but nothing's fail safe."

She closed her eyes tightly and waited for the fallout. Waited for him to bolt from the bed and run like the wind. Instead, he said, "Condoms aren't one hundred percent fail-safe, either. We'll just hope there won't be any consequences. And if there are, we'll deal with it if and when the time comes."

Tori didn't dare ask how he intended to deal with it. She only knew that if she happened to be pregnant, she would love and care for the baby as well as her mother had loved and cared for her. She would tell her child about its father. But would she tell Mitch and face his rejection, the same as her mother?

He lifted her chin and kissed her lips softly, thrusting all the concerns from her mind. "Are you sleepy?"

"Not really."

"Neither am I. Any ideas how we might pass the time?"

He was drawing her in again with only the idle touch of his fingertips stroking her shoulder. "We could go grab a bite to eat in the kitchen," she said, even though she couldn't imagine choking down a bite of anything.

"I'm not hungry."

"Go for a midnight ride in the truck?"

His finger drifted down between her breasts. "Why don't we just go for another midnight ride?"

"But Mitch, it's only been about twenty minutes."

He pulled her over until they were face to face, body to body once more. He pressed against her, making it quite clear that twenty minutes had been more than sufficient. "You're insatiable," she told him.

He palmed her breast. "Downright rapacious."

"Rapacious? How about voracious?"

He slid his hand down her belly and taunted her some more. "Horny."

Tori laughed but not for long. She was too caught up in his caresses to laugh. Too overwhelmed by the fact that he could make her want him so desperately. Too aware that tomorrow would come too soon.

But tonight was theirs—all theirs—and she planned to enjoy it to the fullest.

After last night, Mitch knew every inch of Tori's body, every sweet curve, crevice and furrow. He knew every sound she made when he pleased her, every soft sigh and steady moan. He knew the feel of her hands on him, all over him, and thinking about that now brought his need for her back to life, even if he hadn't slept in over twenty-four hours.

He valued her as a lover, would miss her in those hours before dawn, but he would long for her friendship just as much. That's why he couldn't let her leave until she agreed to see him again.

Determination drove him out the front door that he let slam behind him, startling Tori, who was now standing at the passenger side of Stella's car. He slid his hands deep into his pockets before he did something stupid, like carry her back to his bed to engage her in a little sensual torment until she agreed. But that wasn't the answer right now. She needed to know that this wasn't only about sex. Not by a long shot. How he was going to express that, he had no idea. He'd just have to wing it and wish for the best.

"Need any help?" he asked, realizing he was a little late in making the offer since her bags were already positioned in the trunk. His fault, since he'd stayed way too long in the shower, hoping she might change her mind about joining him after she'd refused the offer. He'd begun to sense the distance she was putting between them long before she'd left his room to pack.

She smiled but it faded fast. "I've got it all. Thanks."

He'd never noticed the flecks of gold in her brown eyes until now, or how the highlights in her brown hair took on the appearance of fire in the sunlight. So much he hadn't noticed and he wanted more opportunities to correct that. "Are you sure you don't want me to take you to the airport?"

"You're needed more here. Buck told me you're all about to saddle up and move the herd."

"I could take a couple of extra hours." Man, he sounded almost desperate. Maybe he was. "The boys won't be back from church until lunchtime."

"That's okay," she said. "Stella needs to pick up some things in the city that she can't get here."

He clenched his jaw tight against protests he wanted to issue over her stubbornness. "Fine. But before you go, we need to talk about when we're going to see each other again."

She leaned back against the car and toed a rock with her sneaker. "I really don't think that's going to be possible."

Damn her resistance. "Sure it is. I either come there or you come here a couple of weekends a month. If money is a problem, I'll buy you a plane ticket."

Her gaze shot to his. "It's not the money, Mitch. But there is a problem."

"What?"

"I've been in a long-distance relationship before. It doesn't work."

"We could try it. It might work for us."

"Yes, it probably would work for you, but not for me."

"I don't understand what you're saying, Tori."

She released a slow breath. "I don't want to be your weekend girl, Mitch. I don't want to end up like Mary Alice, spending the next nine years of my life in a relationship that's never going to go anywhere."

How could he explain that she was nothing like Mary Alice? How could he tell her that she'd meant more to him than any woman he'd been involved with in his thirty-three years? "What do you want from me, Tori?"

"Nothing, Mitch. I don't want anything from you. But I might if we stay involved and I know that scares the hell out of you."

Mitch couldn't deny that. He also couldn't deny he didn't want to lose her completely. "If you mean marriage, you know how I feel about that."

"Oh, yes. You've made that clear as glass."

Turning away, she opened the door but Mitch closed it with his palm before she could climb inside. "Tori, I'm asking you to think about it. You don't have to answer me now."

She faced him again and framed his jaw in her palm. "Yes, I do have to answer you now. And the answer is no. I'm already halfway in love with you, and I don't want to go all the way alone. I don't want my life to be full of goodbyes. So let's just leave it at this." She stood on tiptoe and kissed him as gently as her touch. "I'll send you a copy of the article when I'm through with the final draft."

Still reeling over her declaration, he didn't know what to say. Could he really offer her more than his time in bits and pieces? Could he even consider committing to her? Right now, he wasn't at all sure, so he offered her the only thing he could until he sorted everything out. "You don't have to send the article, Tori. I trust you."

She looked as if he'd given her his entire ranch. "I won't let you down."

She already had, but it wasn't her fault. It was his.

"I have something for you," she said, then pulled a brown clasp envelope out of her back pocket. "Here. But don't open it now."

Mitch took it in his hand and turned it over. "What is it?"

"The picture you took of me in the office."

Damn. "When did you get it developed? *Where* did you get it developed?"

"Stella let me in the drugstore yesterday morning before they opened. I used their equipment."

Man, that was the worst move Tori could've made. "What did you do with the negative, because I don't have to tell you what could happen—"

She patted his arm. "I destroyed it, so don't look so worried."

Something else was also weighing heavily on his mind and he needed to get it out in the open. "You will tell me if you're pregnant, right?"

"We've got to go, Tori," Stella called from the driver's side.

Tori consulted her watch. "She's right. I've got to go. Bye, Mitch. It's been great." Without another word, she slid into the car and closed the door.

It's been great? How many times had he said that to a woman before he sent her away to resume his solitary existence? He was getting a bitter taste of his own medicine, and it burned like acid all the way to his gut.

Angry at Tori over her casual dismissal, at himself for not being the kind of man she needed, Mitch spun around and headed for the house, determined not to watch her drive out of his life. But as if he'd lost command over his will, he turned and leaned a shoulder against the rock support on the front porch. Stella pulled the sedan out of the circular drive and headed away, then stopped abruptly.

When the passenger door opened, Mitch believed Tori had changed her mind. Believed she was coming back to tell him that she didn't want it to be over. At the very least, coming back for one more kiss. Hell, he didn't care why, just as long as she did come back.

All his hope dulled when she exited the car with camera in hand and snapped a picture of him, favoring him with a sweet smile as his final keepsake.

Mitch remained in the same position until the car disappeared from view, the ache that he'd had since that morning growing more intense with each passing moment. But this time it was centered in his chest, right around the neighborhood of his heart.

"Are you going to tell him if you're preggers?"

Avoiding Stella's scrutiny, Tori continued to stare out the side window at the passing scenery on the interstate, what there was to see aside from billboards and the occasional fast-food joint. "I hope I have nothing to tell."

Stella turned down the radio, a good thing since the love song was greatly aiding in Tori's temptation to cry. "He has a right to know."

"And I have a right to live my life as I choose, so butt out."

"My, my, you're testy. I bet you are pregnant."

Tori sent Stella a look as sour as her stomach. "I could be premenstrual. Have you considered that?"

"I guess that could be it, but I don't think it's likely."

"You sound like you want me to be pregnant."

Stella took one hand from the wheel and patted her belly. "Misery loves company."

Miserable was exactly how Tori felt at the moment, and she didn't welcome any advice from her friend or anyone else, for that matter. "Look, if I did happen to be pregnant, I don't see any reason to involve a man who doesn't want kids or marriage or anything that even remotely resembles commitment. It wouldn't be fair to subject my child to that."

"Mitch isn't like your father, Tori. I know he'd want to do the right thing. And if you dig down deep past all that pain you're in now, you'd know it, too."

Tori shifted to one side as far the seatbelt would allow. "What is the right thing, Stella? Marrying only for the sake of a baby?"

She saw a flash of hurt cross her friend's face. "Bobby and I married because we love each other. The baby only sped things up a little."

How could she have been so careless with her words and Stella's feelings? "I didn't mean you and Bobby. I know you love each other. But Mitch doesn't love me."

"Did you ask him?"

"I shouldn't have to ask. I did tell him before I left that I was falling in love with him."

Stella's eyes went wide as the wheel. "What did he say to that?"

"Not a thing, and there's my answer."

"Maybe he's scared, Tori. Bobby nearly swallowed his tongue before he got out the 'love' word the first time."

Tori was terrified. "Love's a scary business, especially where Mitch is concerned. I'm not even sure he's capable of it."

"Oh, he is. It's just going to take the right woman, and I honestly believe that could be you."

If Tori could really believe that, then she would have agreed to see him again. She would have returned to Quail Run on weekends, showed him the sights of Dallas and made love to him as often as she could. But he'd given her no hope of that ever happening. He'd given her no promises. And hopefully, he hadn't given her a child, even though, under different circumstances, that would be the greatest gift of all.

"Speed up a little, Stella," she said. "I'm going to miss my plane."

"You're going to miss Mitch Warner, Tori. You won't be able to escape him, even when you get home."

"I have too much work to do on the article to think about him."

Even before Stella snickered, Tori realized how ridiculous that sounded. "Considering the story's about him, that's going to be tough, Victoria."

Regardless of what had transpired between them, Tori vowed to do the best work she had ever done. She was professional enough to paint a favorable picture of the man, even if he'd considered her only a convenience. Even if he happened to be the man she loved and could never have. He was still a good man. And no one knew that better than Victoria Barnett.

He lives in obscurity in Oklahoma with his grandfather who calls him Gus. The town folk consider him the consummate community leader. To see him on the street, he appears to be a classic contemporary cowboy. But in reality, he's a Harvard-educated rancher whose roots run deep in a political dynasty…

And he was going to be a father.

That morning, Tori had taken three tests to confirm what she already knew—she was pregnant. As her mother had done before her, she'd traded common sense for charisma in the arms of a commitment-phobic cowboy. Another sad case of repeating history.

She had no idea how to tell him. Or even if she should tell him, although he did indicate he wanted to know so they could "deal" with it. But what then?

Tori didn't have time to ponder the hows and whys when her boss breezed in, holding the last draft of the article, number five at Tori's last count.

"I think this is almost it," Renee declared, her smile accentuating her apple cheeks. "It's got everything. Great quotes. Local color. Love the pictures. But…"

Tori hated it when people ended a sentence with "but." "What is it now?"

"You're missing a very important aspect, namely a comment from Edward Senior."

"This is about Mitch Warner, not the senator."

"It just won't ring true unless we interview his father."

She could just imagine what Mitch would have to say about that. "I promised I wouldn't involve his father—"

"You don't make promises you can't keep, Tori."

Renee had that look about her, the one that said she wasn't about to budge short of a sudden Texas tornado, signaling certain defeat for Tori. "And how am I supposed to get this interview when the article goes to press in a few hours?"

Renee tossed the draft on the desk in front of Tori. "I've taken care of that. Senator Warner has agreed to give you fifteen minutes."

Tori felt the internal panic button depressing. "When?"

"Now. He's on his way up. Be nice to him."

With that, Renee swiveled on her heels and strode out of the office before Tori could manage another argument.

A few minutes later, Senator Edward Warner arrived in the open door, an impeccably polished statesman and a glimpse of the future Mitchell Warner. Tori had seen him in numerous photographs and on TV, yet the images had not done him justice.

His black hair was painted silver at the temples and his eyes, though not as light as Mitch's, were sky blue. He was slighter in build and probably two inches shorter than his son, yet his air of confidence and palpable control made Tori's office seem to shrink.

Rising slowly from her seat, Tori regained enough composure to extend her hand. "Senator Warner, I'm Victoria Barnett. Thank you for coming on such short notice."

He stepped forward and took her hand for a brief shake. "Very nice to meet you, Ms. Barnett. I do have a plane to catch back to D.C. in two hours, so I don't have much time."

Tori gestured to the chair opposite hers. "Then please, have a seat and I'll explain why you've been asked here today."

He sat and sent her a practiced politician's smile. "It's my understanding you would like some sort of statement from me concerning a feature on my son."

"Yes, that is what my editor is requesting."

"This wasn't your idea?"

"Actually, no. Mitch doesn't..." She studied the paperweight on her desk, hating how ill-prepared she was for this meeting. "I'm afraid your son—"

"Doesn't care to have my opinion."

She finally looked up and found his expression somber. "That's correct."

"Then I assume you know that our relationship has not been on the best of terms."

"That's been common knowledge for some time. But Mitch did mention it to me a time or two."

"That surprises me, considering my son is a very private man. He also has a strong contempt for the media, and rightfully so. Until the past few years, he's spent his life in the spotlight. He was forced to grieve for his mother on national television. My position has left us all open for scorn."

The disdain in his tone disturbed Tori. "Senator Warner, you are under no obligation to say anything at all."

He smoothed a neatly manicured hand down the lapels of his navy silk suit. "If I thought that I could say something to mend my relationship with my son, I'd do it. I'm afraid it's too late for that."

"It's never too late. I only know that whether he admits it or not, he needs you in his life." Two minutes in his presence, and she'd already revealed too much.

"You sound as if you have a personal investment in Mitch's well-being."

How was she going to dig herself out of this one? Honesty was the best course. "I spent quite a bit of time with him during the interview process. I consider him a friend." And so much more. "He's a good man who happens to be in a lot of pain. I don't like to see anyone suffer."

"And you're suggesting that by adding my thoughts to this story, I'll alleviate some of his resentment toward me?"

"It's worth a try."

"I admire your optimism, Ms. Barnett, even if I don't embrace it." He crossed one leg over the other and adjusted his red tie. "If I speak to you off the record, can I trust that you won't repeat what I'm about to tell you?"

Tori pushed the recorder to one side and folded her hands in front of her. "Of course. But again, I don't want you to feel you have to say anything more."

"Normally, I wouldn't. But I've spoken with Mitch's grandfather and he seems to think you have more than a passing interest in Mitch. He also speaks very highly of you."

Tori nearly choked. "You've talked to Buck?"

"Yes. He's been much more understanding and forgiving than Mitch."

"What exactly did he say?"

"He claims that you're the woman who could bring my son around. I might have passed that off as the ramblings of a hopeful grandfather, but after listening to you for the past few moments, I believe he could be right."

Lord, her feelings for Mitch must be flashing like a neon sign across her face. "As I've said, we're only friends. I think Buck would like it to be more, but that's not very likely."

He looked more than a little skeptical. " Mitch could use a friend. Someone who understands why his wounds run so deep."

Tori already recognized the depths of Mitch's wounds. She also realized every story had two sides. She'd heard Mitch's version; she might as well hear his father's since he was willing to provide it. "Okay, then. If you think it will help, I'm willing to listen."

He shifted in the chair, the first sign of a chink in his composure. "I'm assuming Mitch told you he has never forgiven me for marrying only months after his mother's death."

"Yes. He sees it as a betrayal of her memory."

"It's difficult to explain why things happen the way they do," he continued. "Caroline was there to see me through a very tough time in my life. Not only had I lost my wife, I'd lost my son as well."

"And grief drew you both together." Not so different from Tori's and Mitch's connection brought about by their shared sorrow over the loss of their mothers.

"I suppose in some ways I couldn't face the prospect of living my life alone. Maybe that's a sign of weakness, and maybe that held true in the beginning. But Caroline and I have had a good life that's developed into a solid, loving relationship. Unfortunately, it hasn't included Mitch, by his choice."

"Maybe now that you're relinquishing your senate seat, it might be easier to repair your relationship. If you do intend to retire."

"I do, and my reasons have to do with something that is not yet public knowledge." He gave her a meaningful look. "Again, I'm taking a chance by trusting you, but because you obviously care about my son, I believe this is something you should know. Another reason why Mitch and I might never heal the breach in our relationship."

Tori could not imagine what he was about to say, or if she really wanted to hear it. But if it directly involved Mitch, she needed to know. "Go ahead."

"I'm leaving the senate because my wife's pregnant."

Great. Mitch was about to have a sibling and a child. Fine fodder for the scandal machine. "Congratulations. When's the baby due?"

"My daughter should be here in five months."

"A girl? That's wonderful."

He flashed a father's smile full of pride, but it quickly faded. "Caroline is in her early forties, so it's a high-risk pregnancy. But so far everything is going well. I pray that continues."

Tori witnessed sincere concern in his eyes, maybe even a hint of fear. Understandable. He'd already lost one wife; he was worried he might lose another. "I'm sure everything will be fine. And maybe this blessing will be the first step in repairing your relationship with Mitch."

"I'm not sure if or when I should tell him."

Ironic that Tori was in the same boat. "He probably should hear it from you instead of someone else." Advice she should follow, something that was becoming all too clear. "When the press gets wind of this, it will be all over the country."

"I know. I'll have to decide how to handle that soon."

"In the meantime, if you could find something favorable to say about Mitch for this article, that could help open the lines of communication."

When another long span of silence commenced, Tori feared he might not agree. Then he pointed to the recorder near her hand. "Turn that on."

Tori fumbled for the switch, earning a genuine smile from the senator. "Okay, I'm all set."

He settled back in the chair, as if a weight had been lifted from his shoulders. "Mitch is a fine man and I respect his decision not to carry on the tradition of politics in the family. I'm very proud of what he's accomplished, and I know his mother would be as well." He hesitated for a long moment and in his eyes Tori saw the depth of his pain and remorse. "I love him as much as any man could love his son."

He rose from the chair and said, "You may quote that."

Tori swallowed around the fullness in her throat, struggling to keep the threatening tears at bay as she stood. "Wouldn't you rather tell him that in person?"

He released a resigned sigh. "I gave up on convincing Mitch that I've always had his best interest at heart, even if I've made more than my share of mistakes."

"Maybe he'll be ready to listen after the article comes out."

"That would be great. And a miracle. But if he isn't willing to communicate with me, you can tell him for me. All of it. And take care of him."

With that, he was out the door, and Tori was left alone, stunned by his assumption that Mitch would ever consider letting her take care of him. Shocked that he had so easily read and accurately interpreted her feelings for his son, with a little help from Buck and her own inability to hide her emotions.

At least she had a quote she could use to appease Renee. A sincere, heartfelt quote from a father who was suffering as much as his son. But would Mitch welcome his father's words, or would he take exception to Tori including them? She had no choice. This involved her standing with her editor, her job. Possibly better pay and a promotion, something she would need if she were forced to raise her baby alone as well as pay off her debts. Yet deep down, Tori remained hopeful that this would be a catalyst for opening a dialogue between Mitch and his father. An opportunity for both men to heal. Then again, maybe she was being overly optimistic.

The other two decisions she now faced weighed even heavier on her mind—if and when to tell Mitch about the baby, and whether to open the faded envelope resting atop her desk. Right now, she would deal with the latter.

Drawing a cleansing breath, Tori slit the envelope's seal with one shaky fingertip and unfolded the single page. A faded photo dropped onto the desk—a snapshot of her youthful mother and a smiling cowboy. Presumably, Tori's father.

She gripped the letter in one hand while covering her mouth with the other, her vision blurred from tears as she read the information she'd avoided most of her life.

His name was Rick Ballard. He'd had medium brown hair, dark brown eyes and a pirate's smile, a sweet-talker of the first order. He'd hailed from Wyoming and spent his life on the road as a bull rider. One weekend in October, he'd come to Quail Run to participate in the local rodeo and had sufficiently swept Tori's then seventeen-year-old mother off her feet and into his arms. Eventually into his motel bed on their last night together—the night Tori had been conceived.

The final two revelations sent a sob climbing up Tori's throat that slipped out on the heels of her unexpected sorrow.

He had died two months before Tori's third birthday in a

tragic rodeo accident while doing what he loved to do. Before that fateful day, he had never known that Victoria May Barnett existed, because he'd never known about the pregnancy. And her mother had lied to her daughter all those years by claiming it had been careless disregard that had kept him away from his child.

Tori cleared away her shock to read the four simple words closing the letter, a plea for forgiveness.

"I'm so sorry, honey."

Caught in a stranglehold of emotions, Tori swiped furiously at the tears now streaming down her cheeks. She experienced regret over the loss of her father and anger over her mother's deception. And confused. Why hadn't she been forthcoming with the truth? Maybe Cynthia Barnett had been so ashamed that she'd needed to blame her lover. Maybe she'd inherently known that the man she loved was not interested in commitment and she couldn't change that.

Since the letter offered no explanation for her mother's motives, Tori would never know the whys. But she did know two things.

She would forgive her mother and let go of any bitterness. Otherwise, she would end up like a man she knew. And she had to tell that man about their baby. She would not let her own child suffer the same fate of never knowing its father, regardless of what Mitch chose to do with the information.

For the remaining five workdays, Tori would prepare for the article's release the following Monday. That left the weekend open to do what she had to do. Come Saturday night, she would return home to face her past…and her future.

Ten

I love him as much as any man could love his son….

For the third time in the past half-hour, Mitch read the words in total disbelief. He'd received the advance copy that morning by courier and he realized Tori had probably sent it. Yet she hadn't enclosed a note or an explanation. In fact, he hadn't heard a thing from her since she'd left.

"Smart girl, that Tori," Buck said from the desk chair in the den while he surfed the Internet. "She made you look like a saint in that story."

Mitch had no argument about the content of the article…until he'd come upon the quote from his father near the end. He tossed the pages aside and leaned his head back on the tattered sofa. "She didn't have to go to *him* for his opinion."

Buck swiveled the chair away from the monitor and glared. "Didn't you read what your daddy said? He's proud of you, thinks you're a good man and—"

"I read it, Buck."

"But you ain't paying attention."

He knew his grandfather well enough to know he wouldn't let it go until he'd had his say. Well, Mitch intended to have his say, too. "Why shouldn't I believe this isn't just another ploy to win over his constituency?"

"Because he never needed you for that before. And he's about to take his bow. He's not running again."

"He hasn't confirmed that yet. I'll believe it when I see it."

"Believe it. He told me it's so."

Mitch straightened, every muscle in his body taut with both shock and fury. "When did you speak with him?"

Buck shrugged. "Last Sunday, like I've done almost every Sunday for the past fifteen years. He calls me to check on you since you won't give him the time of day."

Obviously everyone he cared about was bent on subterfuge. "Why the hell didn't you tell me this before?"

"Probably because of the way you're reacting right now."

"And you didn't think I had a right to know or any say-so in the matter?"

"No. I can say whatever I please to whoever I please. I didn't live almost eighty years to have a wet-behind-the-ears grandson telling me otherwise."

Overcome by blinding anger, Mitch swept the article off the couch with his forearm. "And I don't appreciate you going behind my back."

Buck bolted from the chair and stood over Mitch, the fires of hell in his rheumy eyes. "You listen here, young man. You might not respect your daddy, but you will respect me. You've been mule stubborn for much too long. If I can forgive him, then you can, too. She was my daughter, for God's sake."

"And she was *my* mother! Tell me one good reason why I should forgive him for not bothering to be at her deathbed, then marrying another woman before his first wife was barely cold in her grave?"

Buck yanked the magazine from the floor and jabbed a finger at the page. "The reason's right here, plain as the nose on your face. He loves you."

Mitch didn't need this. He didn't want to deal with it. For two solid weeks, he'd done nothing but think about Tori, the loss eating at his insides like rust. Now she'd betrayed him by talking with his father when she'd known all along how he felt about that. "Good for good old Dad. Might have been nice if he'd said it to me in person instead of in print for the world to see."

Now Buck tossed the magazine onto the couch. "Good God, Gus. Don't you remember him telling you every time he left you here in the summer? He said it until you got too big for your britches and quit listening."

"And he quit listening to me a long time ago. He didn't listen when I asked him—begged him—to stay when Mom was sick. He ran off to serve his country, as always. We weren't important enough for him to stick around for any length of time."

"You were important to him, Gus. And it was tough on him, leaving you behind to deal with your mama's sickness. But he tried to get back that night. He didn't know she was going to pass before he made it here. None of us knew."

Mitch felt incredibly tired at the moment. Too tired to rehash old recriminations. "We've been through this before."

Buck snatched his decrepit straw hat from his head and crushed it in his hands. "And we'll keep going through it until you get it through your hard head. Your daddy has never stopped loving you, even when you turned your back on him, just like you turned your back on Tori."

Where the hell had that come from? "This has nothing to do with her."

"It has everything to do with her. You're making the same mistakes. Just like you won't admit you love your daddy, you won't admit that you love her either."

Mitch's gut burned and he closed his eyes against the pounding in his temples, the truth of that statement digging at his heart. "You're crazy, old man."

"I might be crazy, but you're a coward."

Mitch's eyes snapped open. "What did you say?"

"You heard me. You're a coward. A yellow, lily-livered coward."

"I'm not afraid of her."

"You're afraid of your feelings for her, dammit," he hissed. "Admit it to me. You love that girl, otherwise you wouldn't be moping around here, biting anyone's head off if they come within fifty feet of you. You're so sick in love you can't even think straight. Hell, if it hadn't been for Rand, you would've shipped sperm instead of software to that college in Idaho."

He would spend years trying to live down that mistake and no telling how many more. "Let it go, Buck."

"Not until you say it."

This time Mitch vaulted from his seat. "I said let it go."

"I'm going to stand here until you say it, or I die in my tracks, whichever comes first. You know I will."

"Okay, I love her!" Mitch blurted. "Are you happy now?"

Buck's grin looked victorious. "Nope. Not until you tell her."

Mitch paced the room, restless with the admission and the knowledge that he'd blown it with Tori. "I haven't heard a word from her in two weeks. The day she left, I told her I wanted to see her again, but she refused."

"Maybe that's because you didn't offer her more than a quick tumble every now and then. That don't set too well with the womenfolk."

Mitch stopped at the shelf and faced Buck again. "What am I supposed to offer her?"

"Marriage."

"You are crazy. We've only known each other a short time." Yet Mitch felt as if he'd known her for years. She certainly knew him better than any woman ever had. She knew him better than any living soul.

"That don't matter, Gus. Why, I met your grandmother on a blind date one weekend and we got married the next, before I shipped off to the army. Your mama went down to college in

Austin, met your daddy her second year, then married him two months later. You came along about ten months after that."

"That's you and my parents, not me. I prefer to wait a little longer before I decide something that will affect the rest of my life."

"You've waited too long as it is. It's time to grow up, Gus. Be a man. Commit to something other than this place cause it won't keep you warm in the winter. Have a few babies, too. I'd like some great-grandkids hanging around before I get too old to take them fishing by the creek."

Mitch held up his hands, palms forward. "Whoa! You're getting way ahead of yourself. I haven't said I'm going to propose, not to mention Tori's not even speaking to me."

"She will, as long as you say the right thing," Buck said with certainty. "By the way, me and Eula are going to get married in the next week or two, so I'll move in with her. That'll give you and Tori this place all to yourself."

A banner day for bizarre news, Mitch decided. "You're serious?"

"Yep. Eula's a good moral woman and I got to buy the package before I get the goods."

"You're marrying her so you can have sex?"

Buck chuckled. "I'm marrying her because I love the woman. Sex at my age is just topping on the cake."

Despite Mitch's determination not to, he laughed. "Congratulations, Gramps. I hope like hell you know what you're doing."

"I do." Buck pointed a bony finger at him. "And if you call me Gramps again, I'll take you down a notch or two. I also expect to be saying congratulations to you real soon. Maybe we can have a double wedding."

Buck's senility had obviously set in. "No thanks. If I decide to get married, I want my own service. And that's a big if." Mitch couldn't believe the words had left his mouth with such ease. He couldn't believe he was actually considering something as insane as proposing to Tori. Now he was getting ahead of himself. First, he had to find her and then convince her to talk to him. That could prove to be an enormous challenge. One he was ready to undertake. Now.

He started to leave the room before Buck called to him, "Where are you going in such a hurry?"

Mitch stopped at the open door and faced his grandfather. "I'm going to go pack a bag so I can head to Dallas."

"She won't be there, Mitch."

Mitch turned to find Bob standing in the hall, baseball cap in hand. "How do you know?"

"She called Stella yesterday and said she was coming here tonight. We're supposed to meet her at Sadler's around 8 p.m. because she's driving in."

"Did she say why she was coming back?"

"You know women, boss. Stella only told me what she thought I needed to know. But I have a sneakin' suspicion she wanted me to pass the information on to you so you'll show up."

"I might just do that." No might about it. He'd be there and nothing would stop him, not even the case of cold feet threatening to work its way beneath his boots.

In a little over eight hours, Mitch would grab some courage and lay it on the line. In eight hours, he'd finally see Tori again, this time in person instead of in his dreams. Eight hours seemed like a helluva long time to wait.

He guessed if he'd waited half his life to find a woman like her, he could wait a few more hours.

"He's not coming."

Stella patted Tori's hand from across the same table they'd occupied the first night she'd met Mitch, only tonight, Janie and Brianne had been replaced by the now-absent Bobby. "Sure he's coming, sweetie," Stella said. "It's only been an hour."

An hour that had seemed like a millennium to Tori. "Now tell me again what Bobby said to him?"

Stella rolled her eyes. "He told him to meet us here at eight, and Mitch said he would be glad to."

"Are you sure that's all Bobby told him? He didn't say anything about me being here?"

"As far as I know, that's all he said. But you know how men are. They don't go into great detail unless it involves sex or sports. If you want, you can ask Bobby as soon as he gets back from the restroom."

As if Bobby would really tell Tori if he'd slipped up and mentioned her appearance. She rested her cheek on her palm and glanced around the crowded bar. If Mitch happened to come in, she would have a hard time seeing him immediately among the local masses. And if he had wandered in earlier and seen her, he might have left before he'd been discovered. That just made her plain depressed.

"I've got an idea on how you can pass the time, Tori," Stella said.

Cry? That's exactly what Tori wanted to do at the moment. Her roller-coaster emotions were threatening to leave the track for the umpteenth time in a week. "Maybe count Carl's chest hairs spilling out from his T-shirt?"

Stella yanked the spiral lock of hair Tori had been twisting like an old-time washing machine wringer. "You should sing. You know you want to."

Oh, sure. Like she really had something to sing about. "No, thanks. And might I remind you, it's Saturday night. Karaoke's on Friday."

"Carl would probably make an exception. You were really popular the last time you performed. Besides, it would help you to relax."

Tori let go a mirthless laugh. "Singing in front of a jam-packed room is not my idea of relaxing, especially in my nervous state."

At that moment, Bobby returned to the table, saving Tori from having to further argue the no-singing point with her best friend. For once, she was glad to see Stella's other half.

He hitched up his pants, yanked back his chair and dropped into it. "I don't think he's coming, girls."

Tori was no longer glad to see Bobby Lehman, even if she did agree with him. "I just said the same thing a minute ago."

"You want Bobby to go call him, Tori?" Stella asked.

Frustrated, Tori slapped one palm on the table, rattling Bobby's beer bottle and startling the couple. "I feel like I've been thrust back into high school study hall when everyone passes notes. I should've just gone out to the ranch and taken my chances instead of coming here."

"Why didn't you?" Stella asked.

Good question. "I guess I thought this was a more neutral place, in case he decided to slug me for sticking his dad's quote in the story."

Stella looked mortified. "Mitch would never hit a woman, Tori."

"I know that. I meant in case he wants to give me a large piece of his mind." He already owned a large piece of her heart.

Bobby streaked a hand over his square jaw. "Yeah. He wasn't too thrilled about that."

Panic gripped Tori. "You talked to him about it?"

"I kind of overheard him talking to Buck. He'll get over it eventually."

Eventually. Maybe by the time their child turned twenty-one, if she ever had the opportunity to tell him about the baby. "I wouldn't bet on it. He tends to hold grudges." One of the few faults Tori had discovered, but a major one, especially if he turned his resentment on her.

So far nothing was going as planned for Tori tonight. And it only got worse when Carl tapped the microphone and said, "Listen up, people. By special request, you're about to enjoy an encore performance by Tori Barnett doing a little Patsy Cline number! Get up here, little lady, and sing!"

Tori now understood the whole grudge thing. "Stella, if you weren't in such a delicate state, I'd ask you into the parking lot."

She had the gall to laugh. "Oh I'm so sure, Tori, since you're so tough."

Tori didn't felt tough at all. In fact, she felt fragile and frightened, void of confidence in her singing or anything else, for that matter.

The chanting commenced, rumbling through the crowd until Tori was forced to stand and answer their pleas. On her way to the stage, she gave Stella a look that said this was not over.

While Carl put on the music, Tori adjusted the microphone and cleared her throat. If she'd known what Stella had been up to, she would have requested another song. But it was too late to even consider that as the intro began to play.

Tori admitted the song was very appropriate. After she told Mitch about the baby—if she had the chance to tell Mitch—she might only have her sweet dreams of him, forced to start her life anew without his support or the prospect of his love. At least she would have a special reminder in her child, hopefully the best part of them both.

When her cue came, Tori belted out the lyrics as if she had all the strength the world. Sang as if her life depended on the act. And cried despite her efforts to avoid that very thing.

She closed her eyes, willing her voice to remain steady as the tears rolled down her cheeks and onto the red sweater she'd worn the first night she'd met her stubborn cowboy. She didn't bother to brush them away, didn't care who might notice.

This might have been her mother's favorite song, but right now Tori sang to Mitch Warner—wherever he might be.

Standing back at the corner of the crowded bar, Mitch watched Tori give another heartfelt performance. She wore the same clothes and sang the same song from that first night he'd laid eyes on her. But this time, the feelings she stirred deep within him had nothing to do with lust and everything to do with his love for her. He wasn't accustomed to having his control sabotaged by emotions, yet he had no will left to fight it. He was totally unarmed and ready to surrender. From now on, she would call all the shots.

Several patrons greeted him, but he didn't respond beyond

an occasional nod. He moved closer to the stage to get a better look, concerned when he thought he saw moisture dampening her flushed cheeks. Yet her voice remained clear, almost reverent, and now that he knew this had been her mother's favorite, he assumed that was the reason for the tears. But she hadn't cried before, and that led him to believe it could be more than bittersweet memories causing her turmoil.

Seeing her standing there in the spotlight, her sorrow bared for everyone to see, he wanted to go to her and hold her, protect her, yet he had no call to interrupt at the moment. He wasn't even sure she would welcome the intrusion. But when her voice faltered and she stopped before the song's end, he elbowed his way through the muttering crowd, practically shoving several people aside, strode to the stage and caught her hand in his.

She opened her eyes and stared at him, as if she didn't quite believe he was real. When she didn't move, he clasped her waist, pulled her from the platform and into his arms.

They held each other as the music continued, danced as they had that first night together, clung to each other, this time driven by a closeness they'd established during their time together, not chemistry. Mitch recognized their relationship went far beyond desire. Far beyond anything he'd ever expected.

When the original version of the song began to play, several couples drifted onto the dance floor. Mitch didn't care if the whole town decided to three-step. He couldn't imagine letting Tori go, not yet. Not until he felt her continued tears bleeding through his shirt, where her cheek rested against his chest.

He sought her ear and whispered, "Let's get out of here."

She nodded and he took her hand, guiding her toward the exit through the gawking crush of people. On the way out, they passed by Bob, who gave Mitch a salute, and Stella, who grabbed Tori's hand, winked, then let her go.

By the time they reached the door, Mitch was determined to get as far away from this place as possible. He steered Tori toward his truck, opened the door for her and helped her up into the cab, amazed when she didn't ask where he was taking her. He climbed in behind the wheel and shot out of the parking lot, sending a gravel hailstorm in his wake as he sped down the highway toward home.

He tugged Tori close against his side and let silence prevail for the time being. When he arrived at his destination, then they could talk.

After pulling up the drive that led to the old house, he diverted to his right and traveled down the makeshift road leading to the creek. A full moon had risen over the open field, guiding him to the spot that had served as his refuge on more than one occasion, including the day his mother had died. If he needed to come to terms with his feelings for Tori, and reveal them to her, this was the logical place to do it.

After putting the gearshift into Park, he slid out of the truck, rounded the hood and opened Tori's door. Again she didn't refuse his offered hand or his direction, as if she totally relied on his guidance.

He led her to the back of the truck, yanked down the rusty tailgate then seated her there. He stood before her, both her slender hands wrapped securely in his. The moonlight cast Tori's face in gold, a face that Mitch wanted to see every day for the rest of his life. He'd never wanted anything so damn bad. Not his degree. Not his business. Not even his freedom.

But first, he needed to find out what had her so sad, and he hoped like hell it didn't have anything to do with him.

Tori focused on their joined hands, still silent. At least her tears had dried, but that did nothing to alleviate Mitch's concern.

"What's going on, Tori?"

She blew out a shaky breath but failed to look at him. "It's been a tough two weeks."

"I know. I've missed you." More than he'd missed anyone since his mother's death.

"I've missed you, too" she said, keeping her head lowered.

"Tori, look at me." When she complied, he continued. "When I found out you'd be there tonight—"

"Bobby told you?" Both her tone and expression reflected her surprise.

"Yeah. Didn't you know that?"

"No. I asked him not to and he said he wouldn't. I was afraid if you knew I'd be there, you wouldn't come because of the quote from your father in the article."

"I'm not going to lie to you, Tori. I was pretty mad at first since I didn't understand why you did it."

She raised her eyes to his. "I did it for you."

He brushed a strand of hair from her cheek. "I know. And I appreciate that more than you know."

She looked genuinely pleased, and as pretty as Mitch had ever seen her look. "I think you should try to work it out with him," she said. "It's important, especially since I've recently found out my father never knew about me. And I'll never know him because he's gone. He died when I was three."

He felt her pain as keenly as if it was his own. "You read the letter."

"Yes. That's why I think it's important you reestablish a relationship with your own father. He's all you have."

"I realize that now," he said. "But before I deal with that, I have a few things I need to say to you."

Her gaze drifted for a moment and then came back to rest on his eyes. "I need to say some things to you, too. You can go first."

Mitch had every intention of going first, before he lost his courage. "You're going to have to bear with me because I don't have a whole lot of experience with this kind of thing."

"You're a smart guy, Mitch. And articulate. I'm sure you can handle it."

"Just a few simple words from a simple man, Tori. That's all."

"I'm listening."

He tightened his hold on her hands to anchor himself. "Since I left college, I've carefully calculated my life, planned everything down to the last detail. But I've recently realized some things throw all those plans off course."

"I know what you mean. Sometimes things just happen."

"Yeah. I sure as hell didn't plan on you. I didn't plan to stay up at night for two weeks, dealing with this pain I didn't understand. I sure didn't plan to pick up the phone at least a hundred times to call you before I decided that wasn't a good idea."

Now she looked hurt. "Why wasn't it a good idea?"

"First, you told me you didn't want to see me anymore. Second, I didn't know what I wanted from you until today."

"What do you want from me, Mitch?"

"To be with you, and not only tonight." He tipped his forehead against hers. "I can't stand the thought of you walking away and never coming back. I don't think I can take that a second time."

She released a small sob and bit her lip, he assumed to halt another round of tears. He planned to kiss those away eventually—if she let him after he said what he needed to say.

He was down to the wire. The moment of truth had arrived—a moment he'd never thought to confront. "I love you, Tori. God knows I didn't want to, but I do."

Tears threatened at the corners of her eyes but she blinked them back. "Are you sure?"

"It's real, Tori, and I don't want to let it go. I don't want to let you go."

"But there's so much we have to deal with. You're here, I'm in Dallas."

"Marry me and we'll live wherever you want to live." There it was, and not so difficult after all. Not when it was so right.

When she tugged her hands from his grasp, she might has well have knifed him in the gut. "What did you say?"

"Marry me, Tori. Be my wife. I would be honored to be your husband."

"Do you realize how crazy that sounds, Mitch? What are people going to say since we've known each other for such a short time?"

"I don't give a damn what anyone has to say about it, except for you."

She spun a lock of hair around her finger. "First, let me say what I have to say to you. Then we'll see if your offer still stands."

Fear momentarily immobilized Mitch. Fear that he'd screwed everything up by his unwillingness to acknowledge his feelings until now. "I don't think you could say anything that would change my mind. Unless you don't love me."

She dropped her hands to her lap. "Oh, I love you all right."

"But only halfway?"

"All the way. That's not the problem."

Relief reared its head. But frustration and impatience attacked him all at once. "Then what the hell is it?"

"I'm pregnant."

Mitch waited for the urge to run. Waited for the cold sweat, the burning in his gut. It didn't come at all. In fact, what he experienced at the moment felt a lot like pride and joy. "When did you find out?"

"Earlier this week. Actually, the day I met with your dad. That's why I'm here tonight, to tell you."

The same old mistrust came home before he could stop it. "Did you tell him?"

She frowned. "Of course not. I wouldn't tell anyone without telling you first. Even Stella doesn't know. She thinks I'm here just to see you again."

Mitch rubbed his chin and grinned. "I'll be damned."

"I'll be damned? Is that all you can say?"

"You know something, babe. I think subconsciously I wanted to get you pregnant. I could've pulled a condom out of my pocket that night in the truck."

"You had a condom with you?"

"Yep, but I also had a woman in my arms that made me lose my mind because I wanted her so badly." He touched his lips to hers. "I still want her."

Tori swiped at her eyes. "I'm so glad you do. I figured you'd be back at the house by now, locking yourself in."

Overcome with a sense of happiness he'd never before experienced, Mitch lifted her off the truck and set her on her feet, pulling her close. "Buck told me he wanted a great-grandchild before he was too old to enjoy one. Looks like he's going to get his wish. Now am I going to get mine?"

He saw pure love shining in her eyes, all for him. "Yes. I'll marry you. Gladly."

"Thank God." He kissed her again, this time more deeply to drive home his feelings for her. "I love you, baby. And I don't want to wait to get married."

"Just when do you propose we do this?"

"Next week wouldn't be soon enough. But I guess we have to make a few arrangements and decisions about where we're going to live."

"I really don't see why we can't live here."

That totally caught Mitch off guard. "What about your job?"

"It seems that news of your story has already created a lot of buzz, even though it's not out until Monday. I've already started getting some offers. I can work freelance, as long as you understand it might mean quite a bit of traveling at times."

"That's fine, as long as I can go with you most of the time. Because babe, from this point on, I don't want to be without you." And he didn't, not even for a minute.

She brushed a soft kiss over his lips. "And I don't want to be without you, either. Besides, it's been good to be back here. I didn't realize how much I've missed the small-town life, even though we will be the latest topic of gossip."

He saw right through her attempts at false humor. "Tori, I'll make sure no one in this town will ever do or say anything to hurt you again."

"You know something? I'm not really worried. When I think about it, there were very few people who didn't accept me and my mom. People like Mary Alice."

Hopefully that would be the last time he had to hear that name, at least coming from Tori's sweet mouth. "You won't have to worry about her. She broke off her engagement to Brady and she's moving to Chicago. Something about going to culinary school, although I can't imagine Mary Alice doing anything that involved getting her hands dirty."

"I'm glad she's decided not to settle for a mediocre marriage." She gave him a smile and a squeeze. "I'm not."

"I want to make you happy, Tori. The whole thing kind of scares me since my example has fallen short."

Her expression went serious. "Mitch, your father explained a lot to me about the reasons why he married Caroline and why he's now retiring. You need to let him explain it to you, too. And you need to really listen with your heart."

"I'll call him tomorrow. I can tell him about the wedding. But I'm not making any promises on how it will go."

"At least it's a beginning."

He lowered his hand to her abdomen, the place that sheltered the child he'd never believed he would have. A child he already loved. "Here's to new beginnings."

Pulling his hand up, she kissed his palm. "And good memories." She sent a quick glance over her shoulder and grinned. "Want to make a few more?"

Mitch returned her smile. "Yeah, but I'm thinking we should go back up to the house and use a real bed. You need to be comfortable."

Ignoring him, Tori hoisted herself into the truck bed and slipped off her jacket. "I'm thinking we should take advantage of the fact that I'm still mobile enough to do it in unusual places. In a few months, that might not be true."

Without hesitation, Mitch hopped up into the bed and covered it in hay, a repeat of that first monumental night together.

"You know what I'd really like," she said as they settled onto the hay.

Mitch cupped her breast beneath the sweater. "Yeah, baby, I think I do."

"Aside from that."

Her mild scolding didn't stop Mitch from lowering his hand to the zipper on those coronary-inducing leather pants. "Yeah, I know all about that, too."

"Mitch, I have to say this now." She pulled his hand up and held it against her heart. "I want a big wedding. The works. Just like Stella's. As long as I don't have to sing."

"I really like hearing you sing. How about at the reception?"

"I can do that." She gave him a mock-suspicious look. "You're not going to make me sing all the time for my supper, or for sex, are you?"

He slid her zipper down. "No, but I will make you want to sing during sex."

She worked his belt buckle open. "We'll see about that. And I'll make a deal with you. If I promise to sing at our reception, then you have to promise to recite some poetry."

He halted the downward progress of her jeans. "In front of people?"

She gave him a coy look followed by a wink. "If you'll at least think about it, I promise you'll be rewarded for your efforts."

"That's a deal." And he sealed that deal with another kiss, another slow, mind-blowing session of lovemaking under the stars with the woman he would soon make his wife.

As he held her in his arms, Mitchell honestly believed he could accomplish anything. Except maybe poetry reading in public.

What the hell. He would consider it for Tori. Anything for Tori.

Epilogue

"Twice or thrice I have loved thee, before I knew thy face or name. So in a voice, so in a shapeless flame. Angels affect us oft, and worshipped be..."

Three days ago, Mitch Warner had surprised the entire congregation by reciting that verse following his wedding vows. Yet no one had been as shocked—or as touched—as Victoria Barnett-Warner.

The ceremony had been held on a perfect November day in the small country church Tori had attended during her youth every Sunday with her mother. Tori wore Mitch's mother's wedding gown, a gift from Mitch, since her own mother sadly never had the opportunity to wear one. The "Fearsome Foursome" had been reunited when Stella, Janie and Brianne served as attendants, escorted by Bobby and Rand, with Mitch's father assuming the role of best man, at his son's surprising request. Proof positive that the healing process had finally begun.

Both Mitch's and Tori's mothers had been honored with white roses and their framed portraits set out on the pews on each side of the aisle. And Buck, dressed in his Sunday best, sans straw hat, had gladly given the bride away.

They'd chosen Sadler's for the reception—which was quickly becoming a tradition in town, according to Carl who had served as musical host, despite Bobby's protests. But Bobby hadn't complained about the medley of honky-tonk songs Tori had sung at Stella's request.

All in all, it had been a grand party, but it paled in comparison to the honeymoon Tori and Mitch now enjoyed.

For the past two days, she'd been sequestered with her new husband in a massive cabin situated in a small country called Doriana, compliments of Marcel DeLoria, one of Mitch's Harvard friends, who just happened to be the king. Yet they hadn't been very hospitable guests, not bothering to leave their accommodations since their arrival. Mitch had assured Tori that as a newlywed himself, Marc understood completely.

Wrapped in a downy-soft red blanket, Tori stood at the window of their comfortable room, wood smoke rising from the rock hearth positioned in the sitting area opposite the ornate king-size bed. She studied in awe the fat snowflakes drifting over the forest surrounding the cabin, the Pyrenees providing a picturesque backdrop rivaling any panorama Tori had witnessed in her limited travels. But her favorite scenery dozed in the bed behind her, naked as the day he was born and as majestic as any mountain. At one time she might have been known as poor little Tori, but now she was truly rich, steeped in a wealth of love provided by a man who adored her and the baby growing inside her. Thanks to him, she had far too many blessings to count.

She also had a very masculine arm snaking around her middle to pull her back against a muscled chest that she'd come to know very well.

"What are you doing up?" Mitch asked in a husky voice.

She wriggled her bottom against him. "I should be asking you that question."

His soft laugh made her shiver. His hand on her breast made it worse. "If you haven't learned by now what that means, then I guess you need a few more lessons."

She turned into his arms and smiled. "If I wasn't pregnant already, I would have been before the end of this trip."

With a flick of his finger, he dropped the blanket from around her, leaving her naked again. She frowned and said, "It's cold in here, Mitch. The fire's dying down."

He slid his hand down her belly and cupped her between her thighs. "I don't think so."

What an insatiable man. Not that Tori was inclined to complain. "Can we at least get back under the covers?"

Sweeping her into his arms, he laid her back on the four-poster bed and hovered over her, giving her his heat. "Seriously, we probably ought to cool off a little bit. I don't want to hurt you."

"You haven't and you won't. But we could try just holding each other for a minute?"

"No problem." He rolled to his back and took her with him, positioning her close to his side in the crook of his arm. "This is one of my favorite parts of married life. Can't imagine how I lived without it so long."

Tori couldn't imagine how she'd lived without him. "You know, we should really think about getting dressed."

Mitch groaned, loudly. "Why? I've kind of enjoyed being naked all day. And all night. Eating naked. Watching television naked."

Tori rolled her eyes. "We haven't watched any television, Mitch. In fact, I haven't even seen a television."

He grinned. "I'll concede that."

"Right now we need to get ready for the party Marc and Kate are throwing for us. Marc's sending the Hummer up the mountain in less than an hour to escort us back. I don't think that would make a good impression, showing up buck naked, not to mention it's freezing outside. And speaking of Buck, why didn't you tell me he married Eula?"

"For the same reason you didn't tell me about my stepmother's pregnancy. He wanted to tell you himself."

"I'm glad your dad told you at the wedding. I'm also glad you've called a truce."

Mitch's rough sigh echoed in the room. "We still have a lot of work to do. A lot of baggage to overcome."

Tori rose onto one elbow and studied Mitch's stoic expression. "He's worried about the risk Caroline's pregnancy poses. He needs your support."

"I'll do the best I can, as long as you're there with me."

"I promise." She traced the outline of his full lips surrounded by a shadow of dark whiskers. An ever-present surge of desire, of need, flowed through her in a stream of warmth. "Caroline asked us to come over for dinner the weekend after we return home."

"I don't even want to think about going back yet."

"I know, but I have several loose ends to tie up."

"And I have to say goodbye to Ray."

Tori gasped. "Oh my gosh! Is he sick? Do you have to—"

He gave her a reassuring kiss on the cheek. "Nothing like that. I'm donating him to a therapeutic riding program for kids with disabilities. The ranch is about fifty miles away. I can visit him any time."

"I thought you said he still has a few good years left."

"Actually, I promised to give him away if I lost a bet."

Another shocking revelation. "What kind of bet?"

"Marc and me and Dharr Halim—you haven't met him yet—wagered we wouldn't marry before our ten-year reunion. Marc blew it and so did I. Dharr's still a hold-out but since he's a sheikh and destined to rule his country, he's bound to have to marry sooner or later. Hopefully before next May."

"And since you lost, you had to give up your horse?"

"Yeah. The thing that meant the most to me. Ray qualified, until I met you."

Tori's eyes clouded with tears, but this time from pure joy. "You know, I didn't realize the extent of your love until now."

He breezed his fingertips along her cheek and studied her with a world of love in his eyes. "How could you even doubt it, Tori?"

"I don't. But you love me more than your horse, and that says so much."

Mitch laughed and hugged her hard. "I guess that does mean a lot, coming from a cowboy."

"A Harvard cowboy," she said, then planted a kiss on his chest. "A very sexy Harvard cowboy."

As Tori worked hot kisses down his torso, Mitch sucked in a hard breath. "Listen, lady, if you keep going, we're not going anywhere for a while."

She lifted her head from his belly and smiled. "I know."

"You're the one who told me our ride will be coming shortly." And if she didn't quit, the vehicle wouldn't be the only thing.

"I guess you're right." She slithered up his body and planted a warm, wet kiss on his mouth. "But I'm suddenly in a very needy state, so we'll be fashionably late. Now show me exactly how much you love me."

He framed her face in his palms. "First, I'll tell you. I love you more than my horse. I love you for giving me our baby. I love you more than anything, even my life. Today. Tomorrow. From here on out, as long as you're willing to put up with me. Now that's not exactly poetry, but it's the truth."

"You're wrong, Mitch. It sounded exactly like poetry to me. And now I'm going to show you just how much I love you."

Mitch reveled in Tori's lack of inhibition as she made sweet love to him once more. Sure, she was more than a little wicked when it came to pleasing him, but Mitch didn't mind in the least. Every angel was entitled to fall from grace now and then, especially *his* angel.

In the past few weeks, Mitchell Edward Warner III had learned how to love, how to forgive and how to accept life's little surprises. Now he intended to prove himself a devoted husband, a better son and a loving father to his own child. By the end of next year, he planned to be pretty damn good at all three.

* * * * *

If you enjoyed
UNMASKING THE MAVERICK PRINCE,
you will love the next book in Kristi's miniseries,
THE ROYAL WAGER.

Don't miss:
DARING THE DYNAMIC SHEIKH
in October 2004!

DYNASTIES: THE DANFORTHS

A family of prominence...
tested by scandal, sustained by passion.

THE LAWS OF PASSION

(Silhouette Desire #1609, available October '04)

by Linda Conrad

When attorney Marcus Danforth was falsely arrested,
FBI agent Dana Aldrich rushed to prove his innocence.
Brought together by the laws of the court, their
intense mutual attraction ignited the laws of passion.
Yet Dana wanted more from this sizzling
hot lawyer—she wanted love....

Visit Silhouette Books at www.eHarlequin.com

SDYNTLOP

If you enjoyed what you just read,
then we've got an offer you can't resist!

**Take 2 bestselling
love stories FREE!
Plus get a FREE surprise gift!**

Clip this page and mail it to Silhouette Reader Service™

IN U.S.A.	IN CANADA
3010 Walden Ave.	P.O. Box 609
P.O. Box 1867	Fort Erie, Ontario
Buffalo, N.Y. 14240-1867	L2A 5X3

YES! Please send me 2 free Silhouette Desire® novels and my free surprise gift. After receiving them, if I don't wish to receive anymore, I can return the shipping statement marked cancel. If I don't cancel, I will receive 6 brand-new novels every month, before they're available in stores! In the U.S.A., bill me at the bargain price of $3.80 plus 25¢ shipping and handling per book and applicable sales tax, if any*. In Canada, bill me at the bargain price of $4.47 plus 25¢ shipping and handling per book and applicable taxes**. That's the complete price and a savings of at least 10% off the cover prices—what a great deal! I understand that accepting the 2 free books and gift places me under no obligation ever to buy any books. I can always return a shipment and cancel at any time. Even if I never buy another book from Silhouette, the 2 free books and gift are mine to keep forever.

225 SDN DZ9F
326 SDN DZ9G

Name (PLEASE PRINT)

Address Apt.#

City State/Prov. Zip/Postal Code

Not valid to current Silhouette Desire® subscribers.

***Want to try two free books from another series?
Call 1-800-873-8635 or visit www.morefreebooks.com.***

* Terms and prices subject to change without notice. Sales tax applicable in N.Y.
** Canadian residents will be charged applicable provincial taxes and GST.
All orders subject to approval. Offer limited to one per household.
® are registered trademarks owned and used by the trademark owner and or its licensee.

DES04R ©2004 Harlequin Enterprises Limited

On sale now

21 of today's hottest female authors

1 fabulous short-story collection

And all for a good cause.

Featuring *New York Times* bestselling authors

Jennifer Weiner (author of *Good in Bed*),
Sophie Kinsella (author of *Confessions of a Shopaholic*),
Meg Cabot (author of *The Princess Diaries*)

Net proceeds to benefit War Child, a network of organizations dedicated to helping children affected by war.

Also featuring bestselling authors...

Carole Matthews, Sarah Mlynowski, Isabel Wolff, Lynda Curnyn, Chris Manby, Alisa Valdes-Rodriguez, Jill A. Davis, Megan McCafferty, Emily Barr, Jessica Adams, Lisa Jewell, Lauren Henderson, Stella Duffy, Jenny Colgan, Anna Maxted, Adèle Lang, Marian Keyes and Louise Bagshawe

www.RedDressInk.com www.WarChildusa.org

Available wherever trade paperbacks are sold.

™ is a trademark of the publisher.
The War Child logo is the registered trademark of War Child.

RDIGNIMMR

For **FREE online reading,** visit www.eHarlequin.com now and enjoy:

Online Reads
Read **Daily** and **Weekly** chapters from our Internet-exclusive stories by your favorite authors.

Interactive Novels
Cast your vote to help decide how these stories unfold...then stay tuned!

Quick Reads
For shorter romantic reads, try our collection of Poems, Toasts, & More!

Online Read Library
Miss one of our online reads? Come here to catch up!

Reading Groups
Discuss, share and rave with other community members!

For great reading online, visit www.eHarlequin.com today!

INTONL04

Silhouette Desire presents

Annette Broadrick's

second book in her new series

The Crenshaws of Texas

The arousing connection between blue-eyed Jared Crenshaw and Lindsey Russell was undeniable from the moment they met. Before he knew it, Jared had woken up in Lindsey's bed, but how had he gotten there? He was certain they'd been caught in the crossfire of somebody's scandalous scheme....

CAUGHT IN THE CROSSFIRE

Silhouette Desire #1610
On sale October 2004

Available at your favorite retail outlet.

Visit Silhouette Books at www.eHarlequin.com SDCITC

Rochelle Alers's

miniseries

continues with

VERY PRIVATE DUTY

(Silhouette Desire #1613)

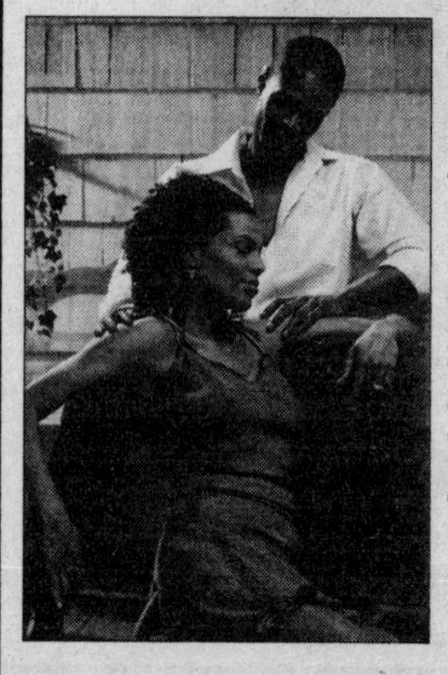

Tricia Parker stepped out of Jeremy Blackstone's high school fantasies and into his bedroom…as his full-time nurse. Could spending time in close—and very cozy—quarters reignite the fire of an old flame?

Available October 2004 at your favorite retail outlet.

Visit Silhouette Books at www.eHarlequin.com SDVPD